BROKEN DREAMS

A Wildfire Book

One

Kelly Horn pulled herself quickly from the swimming pool and shook her short black hair, flicking droplets of water over her boyfriend, Scott Martin, who stood waiting with a dry towel.

Wrapping it around Kelly's shoulders, he gave her a quick hug, and she tilted her head to receive his kiss.

"Hey, it's like kissing a fish," he said.

"Thanks a lot. Are you saying I'm slimy?"

"No, just cold and wet."

"Well, I'll be trading in my swim fins for a formal tonight."

"I won't know you," Scott said, hugging Kelly again.

"If you think you'll have any doubts, I can

come like this." Kelly twirled mischievously, opening the towel to reveal her red tank suit, slightly frayed around the stitching from so much use. Both she and Scott were members of the Clancy High swimming team.

"Naw, you might create a scene. The only mermaid there." Scott scooped a hank of reddish-brown hair from his eyes and grinned one-sidedly at Kelly.

"That gives me an idea for next year's dance theme," Kelly joked. " 'Underwater Ecstasy.' "

"Your jokes are getting worse, but your freestyle's improving a lot," Scott said, glancing at his waterproof diver's watch, which his mother had gotten him last Christmas. "I'm going surfing before the dance, Kelly, so I've gotta get moving."

"Can you at least walk me to the changing room, Aquaman?"

"Sure."

Kelly gazed for one long moment into Scott's dearly familiar face, memorizing — for some reason she couldn't fathom — his characteristically off-center grin, the charming upward tilt of his eyebrows, and the slope of his sea-green eyes, always crinkling with a smile. She threw her arms around him and hugged him hard.

"Hey, what's this all about?" he remarked, clearly startled. "I don't usually get this kind of treatment. We'll see each other tonight, remember?"

"Oh, I don't know," Kelly said, just as baffled by her action as Scott was. "I just felt like it."

They were exactly the same height, so when Kelly looked Scott in the eye, it was straight on unless she wore heels, as she would tonight. But that kind of thing never bothered either of them.

"I'll pick you up at eight, okay?" Scott brushed her cheek with his lips, a gesture Kelly had grown fond of in the last year they'd been going together.

"Okay."

"And remember — wear a dress."

"Very funny." Kelly giggled, watching him saunter through the cyclone gate, shivering at the familiar slope of his shoulders and the lilt of his gait. They knew each other so well and shared so much — namely, sports, a common interest for both of them. They were on the varsity swim and tennis teams and planned to attend Chico State University next fall, majoring in Physical Education. Scott wanted to coach a pro team, while Kelly thought she'd like to try teaching the subject, although she liked the idea of coaching, too.

Sports had always been a big part of her life, which irritated her father, who believed she ought to spend more time studying. But practices were all-important, as was keeping up with sports news, so it wasn't easy or desirable to put aside a great love for tedious old schoolwork.

Fortunately, or unfortunately, whichever way you wanted to look at it, Scott felt about the same way. He constantly had to burn the midnight oil in order to eke out a *B* average and stay on his teams. The couple were often in trouble for staying late at practice — in fact, that was how they had met, one brisk fall evening while Mr. Malmin, the swimming coach, was choosing up teams.

Kelly and Scott had stood side by side, shivering in the deepening dusk. A thick mist swirled around the pool lights and around their feet, causing a riot of goose-pimpled flesh. Kelly remembered wishing she could just get dressed, go home, and sit in front of the fire. She was wondering about Scott, whom she didn't really know, when he spoke.

"We really have to be thick-skinned to put up with this. Can't we go home?"

"Just a minute, Martin. You're new, aren't you?"

"Not to water."

"Just call him Mr. Limpet," Kelly said, giggling. Everyone else joined in, teeth chattering like castanets.

Scott blushed but recovered quickly. "I like that — someone with a real sense of humor." He winked at Kelly.

"That's good — because you're on the same team," Mr. Malmin reported, a pencil held cigarlike between his ample lips. His eyes were buried, raisinlike, in a sun-toasted face, and his thinning hair was covered by a baseball cap turned sideways. "You're all excused."

"I heard you were a champ at Stanton," Kelly addressed Scott with admiration. She always kept up with the sports of area high schools.

Scott draped a towel around his neck, shrugging modestly. "Yeah, I did all right. I'm more coordinated in water than on land."

That didn't prove to be true, however, for Scott was a fearsome challenge on the tennis court, too.

At first, the friendship had seemed to be only that. Kelly considered Scott a good guy to play tennis or swim with. But Scott and Kelly saw so much of each other that gradually other knots tied them together, and they found themselves bonded by a closeness Kelly had never thought possible.

She had never been in love before. And she really hadn't thought about it much, or not as much as many teenagers do, for she was always so involved in other activities that dating was never foremost in her mind. She remembered telling her friends, "If it happens, it happens," and she let it go at that.

"I can just tell by the look in your eyes, it's happened with Scott," her friend, Marilee Cunningham, said one day, when Kelly and Scott strolled off the tennis court, drenched in sweat. Scott playfully swatted her rear with his tennis racket.

Kelly had laughed, perspiration chilling in rivulets down her back as she realized Marilee's words were true. She was crazy about Scott — there were no two ways about it.

That night, Kelly's tennis racket clattered to the cement as Scott put his arms around her, drew her to him, and kissed her for the first time. It was a kiss that lingered in her memory to this day, pressed between pages holding newer ones just as dear to her as that first.

There really was something magical about her and Scott together, she now mused, pulling on her green sweat suit. There was no one who challenged and amused her as Scott did, no one who left a warm and indelible imprint on her heart as he did.

Slinging her damp tote bag over her shoulder, Kelly smiled, thinking of tonight, when she and Scott would be in each other's arms

. . . a good team on the dance floor as well as on the tennis court.

Scott Martin unlashed his surfboard from the rack on top of his beige Toyota and hauled his board down to the northern California beach. He waxed the resined surface in slow, circular strokes, his mind drifting every so often to the way Kelly had looked earlier, popping out of the pool with that dynamite grin of hers.

It was strange the way her image danced to the surface of his thoughts, like a piece of lovely drifting material buoyed by gentle waves. But he should've known she would have this effect on him — from the minute she cracked that silly remark the first time he saw her, he knew she was somebody pretty special. A girl with a sense of humor, smart, and a great athlete. The combination was scary, in a way. Could it be purely coincidental that their interests ran so parallel, or was it that, as his mother suggested, kindred spirits just naturally seek each other out?

Whatever it was, Scott wasn't about to argue or discount any theories, because he was just plain nuts about Kelly. His mom had since commented that Kelly would be his undoing, because Scott spent so much time with her.

"If she wasn't interested in sports, Mom, I wouldn't have time for her," Scott explained one day.

"Too bad she's not interested in getting on the honor roll," she returned drily. "Maybe she could infuse you with some incentive."

"C'mon, Mom, my teams keep me on my toes. If my grades fall, I'm out, remember?"

It wasn't a problem he had to remind his mother or himself of. Grades always haunted him. Trying to accomplish everything at once was difficult. There weren't many hours spent with Kelly on just pure fun. Most of their time together was spent sweating it out on a tennis court or thrashing around in the pool. Scott couldn't remember too many lazy days sitting on a park bench — in fact, there had been only two or three in the past six months.

But Scott came from a family of hard workers. His mom and dad had divorced when he was little, and she had gone back to school, holding down a full-time job at the same time. Mrs. Martin always managed to find time for everything, somehow efficiently fitting her ambitions into a twenty-four hour day, and thus she was equally demanding of Scott and his older brothers Ken and Steven.

Surfing was a sport she disapproved of. She thought it was a nowhere sport, because many people chose to make it their entire life.

Scott didn't look at surfing that way. It was just another sport, but it had special qualities. He liked the freedom of not needing a partner, being the sole manipulator of his ride, balancing on his skill plus a heavy spoonful of chance. An ocean has its own mind and strength. It was like playing against an opponent at some times; at others, it was like being on a team.

But Scott wasn't thinking much about that today as he walked carefully down the narrow wooden steps to the beach. The waves broke high and came in sets — reminding him of tonight and what a good pair he and Kelly were dancing. . . .

Two

"It's gonna be mind-boggling to see you in a dress, Kelly," remarked Marilee Cunningham, Kelly's best friend.

Marilee sat in front of Kelly's Victorian vanity while Kelly unwound Marilee's long, salt-blond hair from thick rollers. Having just tried on some false eyelashes, she was batting them furiously, in an attempt to get used to the way they felt. "I can't believe you and Scott are taking time out for this dance."

"Neither can Scott. He even reminded me to wear a dress. I just hope he doesn't show up in his jogging shorts."

"No telling with him . . . or you."

Kelly glanced over at the celery-green dress that looked oddly out of place in a room decorated with trophies, pennants, and placards. The square, functional furniture contrasted with the ornate vanity, its surface now cluttered with makeup tubes and pots, pushing a group of family photos into one corner.

Yet these differences only pointed out to Kelly the many dimensions of herself reflected in her room. The dress, for instance, was her. She enjoyed dressing up, once she started working on it. And also, once she liked a piece of clothing, she wore it to death. She chose styles that would stay in fashion forever, and her dad was always complaining that she never liked to shop.

The green dress had been hanging in a shop window, belted with a fringed, gold-threaded scarf. "That's the dress," she announced to her father, who protested that he imagined her in something frillier.

"Dad, I am not six years old," she reminded him coolly. "I'm sixteen, and this is the perfect dress for me."

Mickey Horn was continually surprised by his daughter's determination and her certainty about what she wanted out of life, although that shouldn't have come as a surprise — both he and Kelly's mother, Regina, were strong, determined people. Regina, too, knew what she wanted — to be a good wife, a good mother, and a good decorator. She was in New York now setting up the offices of a new client and would be there for a few months.

Kelly spoke to her mom on the phone nearly every day, discussing the latest thrillers they'd read (both were crazy about mysteries) and career paths. They were proud of each other, a fact evidenced by all the memorabilia Kelly had around her room of her mother's accomplishments, side by side with her own.

"Watch where you're sticking those pins, Kelly," complained Marilee.

"Oh, sorry. I was just thinking about my mom. These are the times she gets misty about — first dances and all that."

"Swim-meet victories and Most Valuable Player awards?" Marilee quipped. "My mom would go nuts if she couldn't be in on all my important moments, such as they are." Marilee was being modest — she was class president, director of the play *Charlie's Aunt*, and had written or appeared in almost all the various school stage productions in the past.

"Your first kiss?" joked Kelly.

"Ha-ha. That I keep to myself."

They laughed. "Is Chuck picking you up here?"

"No, at home. Mom wouldn't miss this for the world. She has to take a zillion pictures. These little events will have to suffice until I become the next Neil Simon," she said with a flourish of her see-through scarf, which she planned to wear with her formal.

"Better get an agent, for starters." Kelly giggled.

Marilee wrapped the scarf around Kelly's neck, pretending to strangle her. "Ver-ry funny."

Out of curlers, Marilee's platinum locks reached the middle of her back. She secured a hank of hair with a flowered comb and dabbed blush on her already flushed cheeks and across her freckled nose. "Do I look okay?"

Kelly gave her the once-over and suppressed a giggle. "All except for the high heels and cutoffs — unless you're planning on starting a new rage."

"I'm leaving." Marilee wagged her head in disgust, bumping into Kelly's dad as she flounced out the bedroom door.

"Hey, watch it! Man entering at his own risk. A surprise for you downstairs, Kelly." Her father winked conspiratorially, sending the girls careening down the spiral staircase.

On the hall stand sat a little white box tied with a pink ribbon. Kelly peeled back the several layers of tissue to find a single, perfect, pink rose. The card read: *To Kelly — Here's to another important moment. Love as always, Mom.*

"Wow," breathed Marilee. "How sweet of her." She squeezed Kelly's shoulder. "I'll see you at the dance, kid."

Even though they were the same age, Marilee always called Kelly "kid." Kelly thought maybe it was part of her stage talk.

They said good-bye, and Kelly went directly to the phone to thank Regina.

"Just in case Prince Charming forgets a boutonniere." She laughed.

"That's possible, Mom. You know Scott."

"In his gym shorts only. Never mind — you two have so much in common it's frightening."

"It's nice."

"I understand, believe me. Your father and I know about love, too. Listen, I have to run. Have a good time."

The long-distance connection crackled, reminding Kelly of how far away her mother was. She knew her mom felt it, too. "Bye," she said softly, a lump forming in her throat.

Kelly ate dinner without really tasting it, she was so excited about the dance. Scott hadn't called, though she didn't know why she expected him to.

"He's probably having trouble getting his bow tie on straight," her father joked, his brown eyes surveying her with amusement. He had a slight build, and from the top of his curly head to his sockless feet, Mickey Horn appeared perpetually rumpled, even his eyebrows slightly askew. It was a look, Kelly remembered, from his days as a foreign correspondent for a large metropolitan newspaper. And rumpled-looking he remained, in his only slightly less hectic job as their small town newspaper's senior reporter. He'd taken the job so that he wouldn't have to be away so much, freeing up his wife to pursue her own career. "I always have trouble with those things," he said. "That's when a man needs a mother."

"Or a daughter or a wife?"

"Take your pick."

Kelly knew he said that just to elicit a reaction from her, knowing full well her feelings on stereotypes, so she pretended to ignore him. She ran upstairs and put some music on, then slipped into the green dress, belting it the way she'd seen it in the store window. It was as perfect as she had imagined it would be. With pale green shoes and the gold locket Scott had given her at her last birthday, the whole ensemble was complete, contrasting nicely with her dark hair.

Surveying her reflection in the mirror, Kelly was satisfied.

"You were right, Kelly. The dress is perfect," her father remarked with obvious approval. "I must learn to trust your judgment."

"You must. Stop forgetting I'm all grown-up."

"Isn't Scott supposed to be here by now? I thought we were going to take some pictures." He frowned at his watch.

"He might still be surfing, Dad. He'll arrive shaking seawater out of his ears."

They sat down together in the living room. Kelly got increasingly nervous as she sat through two *Mash* reruns and a special news report — her stomach clenching into a tight knot.

"I'm calling him," she announced aloud, going to the phone. No answer. He must be on his way.

But he didn't come. Kelly memorized every framed painting on the wall — the Gainsborough, the Le Brun, the posters Dad had brought back from European museums. Where *was* Scott? He knew what time the dance started — they'd agreed he'd come over at eight o'clock.

Scott was generally reliable, and Kelly was certain he'd call if he'd been held up. It was now creeping up to nine-thirty.

The phone rang. Kelly tensed, answering it on the first ring.

"For God's sake, Kell, where are you?"

It was Marilee.

"We're . . . not coming right now, Marilee. Scott isn't here yet, and I don't know where he is. I'm worried." Her voice sounded alien to her own ears, the words plunking tonelessly into the receiver like stones.

"What're you going to do?"

What am I going to do? Kelly was suddenly annoyed. The music from the dance filtered through the phone, tantalizing her. She could go on to the dance without him, but what if something had happened to him? "Wait, Marilee. I'm just going to wait here until I hear from him."

Marilee sighed. "Well, okay. I'll call later if you don't show up."

If this was some kind of joke, Kelly would be furious, yet nearly anything was preferable to this silence.

"I don't understand it, Kelly. He wouldn't be this late," her father said. "Shall I call the highway patrol?"

Kelly shook her head, fear coursing through her veins now at the image of Scott lying hurt somewhere. She tried calling his house, but there was still no answer. She called at his friends' homes. Some were at the dance, and their parents hadn't seen or heard from Scott.

Wrapping her light cotton shawl closely

around her shoulders, Kelly huddled on the couch, not speaking, just waiting, her heart thudding so loudly it seemed to take up the entire room. She willed the phone to ring, but when it did, she nearly jumped out of her skin.

Three

Scott couldn't move. He could not feel part of his body, and yet he knew he was hurt. Doctors and nurses bending over him blurred into a gray smudge, their mouths forming words that he couldn't hear. His mind reached backward for something to grab hold of, but it was like grabbing onto a slick, moss-covered cliff — there was no purchase there.

"You understand you've been hurt, don't you, Scott? Now, don't try to move." A male voice faded in and out, as if someone was switching the volume on a radio on and off.

Scott wanted to nod, but something bound his neck, restricting him.

"We're taking X rays to see if there's any dislocation of cervical vertebrae."

Fear overtook him, cold and palpable. "Wh-what happened?" he managed. The gurney whooshed down the hall now, lights flickering above him, stinging his eyes.

"You had a surfing accident. . . ." The words jumbled together with other sounds as they passed through a doorway leading to the X-ray room.

"Kelly . . ." Scott muttered from between cracked lips.

"Your family's been notified. They'll be here soon."

"But . . ."

An image of Kelly as he'd seen her earlier that day came into his mind, and he wondered if his mother would call her. He longed to see her, but then, he didn't know if he wanted her to see him. He had no idea what he looked like. *Maybe I'm maimed,* he worried. He heard one of the technicians say the word *paralysis,* which he hoped did not apply to himself.

But he couldn't feel anything. Maybe it was just shock. . . .

"Scott, it's me, Darren. D'you know what happened to you?"

"No." Scott looked into his surfing buddy Darren Peterson's face.

"A wave creamed you when you went after

your board. I guess you got whapped against the floor. They say you'll be okay."

"My arms and legs . . ." Scott saw the shaking limbs but couldn't feel them.

"Yeah, that'll go away. You'll be good as new," Darren said firmly.

Scott lost all sense of time and place. He might've slept, for the next thing he saw was his mother's small, pinched face swimming before him, sick and pale with fright. She was fighting back tears, he could tell by the set of her jaw.

He tried to tell himself this wasn't really happening. Any minute, he would wake up and find it was a bad dream and wipe the sweat from his brow with relief.

"Darling, the doctors say you'll be fine. They have to find out how badly you're injured. . . ." His mother's lip trembled.

The numbness in Scott's hands tingled, as if he'd sat on them too long. *It'll be better tomorrow,* he decided, pushing back panic. His mother squeezed his upper arm, the simple gesture seeming dear to him at that moment, triggering tears.

"Does Kelly know?" he whispered hoarsely.

"Not yet." His mom whisked a Kleenex out of her purse and dabbed at his eyes. Scott felt like a baby, but he was too confused and hurt to care. "I'll call her in a minute. Your father will be flying in tomorrow."

If I'm here tomorrow, Scott considered gloomily, fresh waves of fear breaking over him — but, strangely, not making a complete circuit through his lifeless limbs.

Nothing in Mrs. Martin's phone call could ease the shock for Kelly. Her words climbed over a knot of tears to tell Kelly that Scott had been in an accident.

"I knew it," Kelly breathed shakily, her body trembling.

"He was surfing," Mrs. Martin went on, "and a wave knocked him over. A neurosurgeon is looking at him now."

Immediately, Kelly visualized television-drama images of accidents — lifeless, rag-doll bodies on stretchers. *But Scott couldn't be like that,* she kept telling herself, even after Mrs. Martin explained that Scott was unable to move.

"He's experiencing spasms, which the doctors think is a good sign," she said hopefully. "And he asked for you."

That was all Kelly needed to hear. "I'll be right there."

Too stunned to cry, Kelly snatched up the car keys, told her father what had happened, and hurried out to the garage.

"Hey, Kelly, wait. My God, let me drive you. You're in no condition —"

"Dad, I'm fine."

But without an argument, she allowed him to pry the keys out of her grasp. For the whole ride to the hospital, images of a healthy Scott flitted through her mind — Scott running and playing and swimming, a guy who could never keep still. His grade-school teachers had always complained about his exuberance, but it had become a great asset later. How could someone so strong and lively suddenly not be that way?

Kelly shook away the thoughts as if they were simply part of a nightmare, which she prayed they were. *He's going to be all right*, she told herself, smoothing the silky green skirt of her dress, thinking how weird it was to be wearing a formal to the hospital.

Mrs. Martin must have thought so, too, for she uttered a surprised little gasp upon seeing Kelly. "Oh, the dance . . ." she mumbled.

"How is he?" Kelly reached for the older woman's hands, long-fingered and white like those in an Ivory soap ad. Her skin was in sharp contrast with her frothy dark curls, even more so at this moment, with every ounce of color drained from it. And her eyes appeared unnaturally huge and round in the small, delicate-boned face.

Mrs. Martin shrugged. "The doctors don't know, Kelly. He injured his cervical vertebrae, which generally means some level of paralysis, they say. He's experiencing loss of sensation from his chest down. But I can't believe Scotty can be like that. He's so strong, he can overcome anything. Why, do you remember that time he broke his leg playing football?"

"This is different, Alice." Mickey Horn tried to make her see the situation more clearly.

"He's going to get over this, Kelly, you'll see," Mrs. Martin insisted.

"Can I see him?"

"You'll have to ask the nurse. He's in Intensive Care, and then they're going to transfer him to a special-care hospital."

At first, Kelly didn't recognize Scott. He was strapped to a strange, circular bed, in which he looked small and wan, and protruding from his head were metal things that resembled ice tongs, which she later found out were called just that. Around the tongs, patches of his hair had been shaven off. The untidy reddish-brown mop was clumped up, and Kelly wished she could comb it for him. His breath made foggy imprints on the inside of the plastic respirator.

Kelly covered his limp hand with hers. "Scott, it's me, Kelly. I'm here for you, and I love you. Just hang in there, okay? They're figuring out what's wrong now."

His eyes, generally full of mischief, stared back at her now with piercing confusion. *My*

God, what would it be like, trapped in your own body? Kelly wondered, her heart aching.

Scott's fingers fluttered against hers, and she looked down to see his hand trying to close around hers. So there *was* hope. She smiled and squeezed her encouragement to him. "You're going to get better, Scott, you really are."

She leaned over and kissed his forehead, which felt cool and yet damp with sweat.

"Time's up," a nurse announced, putting an abrupt end to their brief visit.

Her father was waiting outside the room, and Kelly fell into his arms, burying her face in his checkered shirt. She wanted to cry, but her sobs were caught in her throat.

Dr. Nathan, a neurologist Kelly and the Martins would see a lot of in the weeks to come, was talking to Mrs. Martin.

"He has a low fracture dislocation on the seventh cervical vertebrae, which are the ones here." He indicated the vertebrae in the neck. "Now, we refer to the resulting spinal cord damage by the adjacent bones of the vertabral column, so we call Scott's injury a C7, meaning seventh cervical vertebrae. An injury in the cervical vertabra generally causes dysfunction in the upper and lower limbs. The ice tongs you see penetrate the outer layer of the skull, so weight and traction can be put on it to keep the spine immobilized, so that the cord can heal.

"You must be prepared for the fact that Scott will be disabled in some way, though he shows signs of return already. But recovery is a slow process."

"What can we do?" Mrs. Martin asked, her hands knotted together until the knuckles showed white.

"Not much. Now it's up to the medical team to get him functioning again."

"There's nothing more we can do, Kelly. We might as well go home," her father said.

"I don't want to leave."

"You need your sleep. Scott will want to see you tomorrow, looking cheerful."

She stared at her father as if he was crazy. How could anyone be cheerful at a time like this?

"I know it sounds crazy, but you've got to keep your spirits up. Things are bad enough as it is — Scott can't stand your disappointment on top of his own."

"We'll see you tomorrow, Kelly," Mrs. Martin said.

Kelly nodded and followed her father out of the waiting room and down the endless corridor into the night. One lone star pricked the blanket of darkness — one little twinkle of hope that Scott would be okay, she wished, climbing into the car.

F*our*

The next morning, Kelly was awakened by the insistent ringing of the telephone. In an instant, recalling the events of the night before, she felt guilty for sleeping so long. Her heart tightened, thinking the phone call must be about Scott.

"It's me, Marilee. What happened to you guys last night?"

Kelly propped herself on one elbow. The dance seemed a million years away. In the corner, her green dress was in a heap, the life gone out of it, her green shoes kicked off to either side of the bedroom. So suddenly, without notice, all that had become so secondary, but to Marilee, it was the news of the day.

". . . Chuck and I had the greatest time! You know the band, The Revolutionaries? They were fantastic. . . . At first we thought they were going to be awful, but no way. Lana Biddle and Joe Harris got in a big argument and she threw her flowers in his face, so he stomped out. Wendy Jossi wore these incredible pink shoes with big roses on the toes. And d'you know who got together?" A suspenseful silence followed in which Kelly could not respond. "Marta Baker and Ted Heisler."

"Oh, Marilee . . ." Kelly's eyes filled with tears.

"What's wrong, Kelly? Did you and Scott have a fight or something? I half-expected you two to show in swim fins and snorkels just as a joke. . . ."

"Scott had a surfing accident, Mare. He's . . . paralyzed." The word stuck in her throat, refusing to dislodge.

Marilee gasped. *"Paralyzed? Are you kidding?"*

"No . . . why would I? . . ."

"Will it last forever?"

"No one knows. He can't move his legs and part of his arms and hands. They're moving him to another hospital. He's got to have therapy." She related all this haltingly, wishing it were information that didn't touch her.

"I'm so scared, Marilee. You know how

28

Scott is about sports. He's an athlete, for crying out loud. How does an athlete live with a body that doesn't work right?"

"Now, don't jump to conclusions. Maybe it's not as bad as all that. You know, a lot of people recover feeling in their limbs after this kind of accident. I'll talk to my mother about it." Marilee's mother was a nurse at the Community Hospital. "C'mon, you're always telling me to think positive. What's Scott going to do if you don't keep a smile on your face?"

"That's the hardest thing to do when I see him. But you're right." Still, the immensity of the accident was overwhelming, and there was no way to lessen it.

"How'd it happen?"

Kelly related the story as far as she knew it.

"He's lucky he didn't break his neck," Marilee said.

"That's what the doctor said."

Next Kelly phoned the hospital to learn that Scott had been transferred to the Spinal Cord Injury unit of a medical center forty miles away.

"Do you want me to drive you this morning?" her father offered over breakfast.

Kelly stared at her toast and soft-boiled egg, leaving them untouched. "Thanks. I can drive."

"I'll keep you company?"

She smiled. "Okay."

"C'mon, Kelly, eat something. You've got to keep your strength up."

"I can't eat, Dad. I keep thinking about Scott. . . ."

"Knowing him, he wouldn't want you to miss out on one of his favorite pastimes." Scott had been affectionately dubbed "Bottomless Pit" by Mickey Horn.

The doorbell rang. Kelly answered it, surprised to see Darren Peterson on the steps.

"You already know about Scott?" He looked worried. "I tried to reach you last night, but I guess you'd already left for the hospital. Is he any better?"

"We don't know. They transferred him." She brought Darren up to date. "How did you know about the accident?"

"I was there when he was hurt. A wave crashed down on him when he was going for his board, pushing him to the ocean floor. Me and two other guys went after him and got him to shore. Scott wasn't able to talk about it when he was brought in, of course. He was in shock and couldn't remember what had happened."

Kelly winced, visualizing Scott being thumped around by the water like a piece of driftwood. "Scott's such a strong swimmer," she said.

"Well, I guess nobody's strong enough, sometimes." Glancing at her sideways, Darren suggested, "Hey, look. I was going surfing, but I don't much feel like it now. Can I drive you over to the hospital?"

"Oh, sure," Kelly agreed, knowing her father's previous offer meant putting aside a mountain of work. It would be good to have company on the long drive, too.

When they arrived at the medical center, a physical therapist was with Scott, so Kelly and Darren couldn't see him right away. They sat in the lobby and watched the patients, many of them fitted with the same ice tongs as Scott but sitting in wheelchairs or walking around. Kelly longed to ask them about themselves, but she didn't want to appear insensitive. Her head was full of questions which no one seemed to know the answers to yet.

"You can only see him for a couple of minutes," the nurse instructed. Her wide, inviting smile thawed Kelly, giving vibrations that nothing could be all that bad.

"Hey, Scott, buddy, how's it going?" Darren said as he and Kelly walked into Scott's room.

Scott executed a half-smile, mouthing the word, "Okay." He still had the respirator on, and the ice tongs. Kelly arranged her face into a smile, unable to keep her lips from trembling. She touched his arm and ran her finger up it to see if he was at all ticklish. His fingers moved.

"He moved!" Darren exclaimed.

"Yes, the doctor says that's a good sign," Kelly whispered. "You're going to get better, Scott. You've got to think of that."

Obviously, Darren had only high expectations. "Scott, you'll be roaring around that tennis court in no time. I can't wait to see you on your feet."

Scott tried to nod.

"Darren . . ." Kelly shot him a warning glance. "I think we'd better go." Scott's eyes following her movements made Kelly want to cry. "Scott, I'll see you later. We have to let you rest, but I'll be here for awhile, okay? Love you." She brushed her lips across his cheek, feeling the roughness of his chin where he was starting to get a beard, or "peachfuzz," as she jokingly called it, which always got him mad.

Outside the room, Darren turned to her. "He's a mess, Kelly. Do you think he'll ever walk again?"

"We're all wondering that, Darren. But nobody wants to think he won't. His mom says he's always been strong." Remembering Scott's slack body made tears come to Kelly's eyes.

"Hey, why don't we get a Coke or something?" Darren suggested, and they went down to the cafeteria.

"I can't stand to see him like that," Kelly admitted. "It just isn't him, d'you know what I mean?"

"Yeah, it's scary. I can't imagine him tooling around in a wheelchair like these other people."

"It's a possibility you must be prepared for," a voice said.

Both Kelly and Darren whirled around in surprise. Dr. Nathan, who had attended Scott when he was first admitted, stood over them with his lunch tray. "May I sit down?"

"Sure," Kelly said.

"I was just checking on Scott, as I have two other patients over here at the moment. I'm glad I ran into you, Kelly."

Quickly, she introduced Darren, and Darren explained again how he believed the accident had happened.

"Scott's seriously hurt, and you mustn't expect too much from him. Families and friends do that, you know, without meaning to. It's hard to accept the reality that someone as lively as Scott is going to have a disability of some kind or another for the rest of his life."

"For the rest of his life?" Kelly echoed, feeling numb. "I thought he'd get better, get the feeling back in his arms and legs. . . ."

"Oh, sure, he'll regain feeling, but it's a slow process. He must learn to do everything, almost from the very beginning. He has to learn to feed himself, walk, brush his teeth — all those things we take for granted. It looks like he will have a large measure of return, but then I don't want to give you false hopes. Some quadriplegics end up with more function in the legs than in the hands, though I don't imagine that will be Scott's case." The doctor, who reminded Kelly of a Mr. Potato Head with his thick black eyebrows and button eyes, attacked his jello salad. "I'll give you some literature about spinal cord injury so that you can better understand what Scott's going through, Kelly, and what might be happening to him while he's in here."

"Thank you."

Unfortunately, none of Kelly's fears were put to rest by Dr. Nathan. Instead, they seemed to multiply, popping up like little toadstools after a rain.

Kelly felt strangely cold as she slid into Darren's car. They drove the forty miles home in relative silence, each left to anxious thoughts. When they reached the city limits, Darren asked, "Do you want to drive by the beach? I haven't checked the waves today."

Kelly winced.

"Oh, sorry. I didn't mean . . . "

"No, it's okay. I have to look at the ocean again sometime."

To Darren, the ocean was a way of life. He couldn't go a day without checking the surf, but now Kelly realized it signified pain to her. The waves beating against the rocks looked ominous, and their bone-cracking sound reverberated in her head, making her tremble.

"This is where it happened." Darren stopped the car and got out.

"Why are you showing me this?" cried Kelly, covering her face with her hands.

"Because I thought you'd be interested. Sometimes your imagination paints a worse picture than reality. I saw Scott waxing his board here." He pointed to a sandy area on the cliff. "We talked for a few minutes before we went into the water. Next thing I knew, he was being thumped around by the waves, and his board was up near the rocks."

"His leash wasn't attached to him?" Kelly was referring to the leash that is attached to a surfboard and which the surfer wears around his wrist.

"No. Somehow, it got away from him. He was going after the board when it happened."

"I'm glad I wasn't here," Kelly whispered, although she would have liked to have comforted Scott, held him in her arms as she wished she could do now. *Will we ever really touch again?* she wondered, experiencing a sudden chill.

"What do you think about Scott being disabled for the rest of his life?" Darren asked brusquely.

"What do I *think*? I've barely had time to think about it, Darren," Kelly returned. "I'm really scared. Right now, we're faced with unknowns — nobody knows how much he'll recover, so how do I know what to think? I only know that I love him and want him well, that's all."

"He's a good guy. I always admired him. I can't believe that a surfer who's such a top-notch swimmer like Scott can get hurt like this."

"It doesn't have anything to do with his expertise," Kelly said with anger. "You can be super strong and knowledgeable, but the ocean's bigger and stronger than you are. Scott always thought he was invincible, but I guess this proves he isn't."

They watched in silence as a group of surfers readied themselves for a wave. Some backed off, and two rode it in, whisking along the inside curl for a perfect ride.

Kelly imagined Scott's muscular body on one of those boards, saw him crouch and duck and dance with the board, and it hurt to think that he might never get out there on a wave again.

"How's it going, Kelly?" Steve Shadle, a friend of Scott's, asked. "Scott any better? Sure took a tumble."

Some others crowded around, the drops from their wet suits forming little indentations in the sand.

"We're not sure how he'll be," Kelly informed them.

"Tell him to get back out here as soon as he can!"

"Sure. I will." Watching the guys trek single file down the rock staircase to the beach, Kelly asked, "What would you feel like if you couldn't surf again, Darren?"

"Ugh! I think I'd go crazy. Surfing's just so much a part of me. I sit in class and think about getting out here and riding a wave. I don't know if I'd want to live."

"That bad, huh?"

"Yeah. I don't know if Scott feels like that, but I would. It's too important to me. It could become more important to Scott than it is now, if it's taken away, Kelly. A hundred times more important."

The thought, coupled with the screech of gulls overhead, made her shiver.

Scott fought the woolly layers of sleep that kept pulling him under, coming to the surface to find his limbs still, as if they didn't belong to him. In his dreams, he visualized himself running, catching a fly ball, tossing it to a pitcher. Perfect catch. And then his legs flutter-kicked down the length of the pool, racing Kelly, her arms rising cleanly in rhythmic arcs in front of him. But his legs weren't attached to his body. As though they had their own life, separate entities, they raced off without him.

And then the nightmare: the wave that bulged behind him as he lunged for his board. He was swimming (that much he remembered clearly), the wave arched high above him, and he thought, *It shouldn't break so quickly*. It gathered a thundering force that broke like a ton of bricks — crashing down on his tender weight, grinding him into the ocean floor. He imagined the rest because at that point he must have blacked out — his body twisted, bent like a straw, and spewn out somewhere. The next thing he remembered was being brought up the rocks on a stretcher, his body a stranger to him as it had been ever since.

He was grateful that Kelly hadn't been there to see it happen, although he had wanted the comfort of her arms about him more than anything. But he couldn't bear her pain as well as his own.

He had to get well, there was no question

about it. Kelly wouldn't be able to put up with a boyfriend who couldn't do anything.

But, as she said earlier, the movement of his hands was a sign, a promise. He would get better, he knew it.

Scott fell back to sleep, into the wonderland of dreams where he could still move and run and play and reach up and wrap his arms tightly around Kelly.

$F\underline{\mathit{ive}}$

Kelly trudged up the hospital stairs from the cafeteria, balancing cups of coffee, feeling a million years old. The last few days had passed in a dream, and she wasn't even sure what day it was now. Usually, going to school made her aware of the days in the week, but with all her thoughts focused on Scott, all her daily schedules and plans fell by the wayside, and she hadn't been able to bring herself to go to school since the accident.

Mr. Martin was in the waiting area, glaring at his ex-wife as he paced back and forth across the polished linoleum.

"What if he never walks again, Alice?" he sputtered, his handsome features, so like Scott's, turning beet-red, his eyes filling up in spite of his clenched expression. He was tall, angular, and tanned, as Scott was. Kelly remembered Scott telling her he worked as an archeologist, digging up Indian remains in the Southwest. Scott had many interesting artifacts decorating his room, copies of the arrowheads and pottery that he had helped dig for on summer vacations in the desert.

"It's out of our hands, Jerry," Mrs. Martin whispered, her lips coming together to form a colorless line. "You can't fight it."

Kelly heard the accusation in their voices, wondering how two married people could sound so disappointed in one another. It was strange that while a tragedy such as this brought people closer together, it also dredged up a lot of old anger. Jerry Martin looked defeated, sorrow etched deeply into his tired face. Alice Martin, on the other hand, looked smaller than ever before next to the towering frame of her ex-husband. Kelly felt sorry for them both.

"Mr. Martin, we're doing our very best for your son." Dr. Nathan provided the voice of reassurance. "He may not be able to do everything he did before, such as play tennis or football, but he'll be able to swim and engage in many other activities, I'm quite sure. But he won't be able to do anything overnight. He has two or three years of work ahead of him."

Kelly and Mrs. Martin exchanged long looks. "I can't imagine Scott giving up sports," Mrs. Martin pronounced gravely.

"Scott isn't going to give up anything," Kelly said.

"Now, Kelly, remember, we must be realistic," Dr. Nathan admonished. "He's one of the lucky ones — his paralysis is incomplete, but it doesn't mean we can look forward to miraculous, instant recovery. It just doesn't work that way. Rehab is a long, arduous road."

"I guess we can only pray for miracles," Mrs. Martin breathed tearfully.

"Meanwhile, sleep is what the doctor orders for *you*, Mrs. Martin. You have to rest," Dr. Nathan said firmly.

Mrs. Martin had been dividing her time between the hospital and home, and the staff had even arranged a bed for her at the hospital.

"I'm going to say good-bye to Scott." Kelly walked down the hall to Scott's room. *If only the clock could be turned back,* she thought longingly.

The room was full of flowers and cards, some of which had fallen down. Kelly propped them back up, facing Scott.

The bed Scott was in allowed him to be tipped forward and backward and turned from side to side. It was necessary to change his position every two hours to avoid pressure sores.

"How are you feeling?" Kelly asked, touching his cheek, which felt warm. From the material Dr. Nathan had given her, she learned that a person suffering from a spinal cord injury has trouble with regulation of body temperature and is unable to take anything to control it.

"How would you feel if you were trapped in one of these things?" Scott answered, scowling.

"Awful, I'm sure." She fought back tears at the sight of his boyish, frightened face and the sound of his ragged breathing.

"Let's just say I'd feel a lot better if I was playing in a tennis tourney right now. What I want is to be able to!"

"You will be able to, Scott." Kelly tried to sound encouraging.

"Don't be dumb, Kelly. Please don't be like everyone else around here. They've been telling me I'll be okay ever since I came in here. But nobody can guarantee I'll walk again, and nobody knows how much recovery I can expect. It is an 'incomplete' paralysis, which means I'm not a total basket case."

"Scott, don't talk like that . . . "

"Like what, Kelly? Do you realize what this means . . . to me . . . to us?" Their eyes met and held for one long, excruciating moment, each knowing what the other was thinking.

"Does it still hurt?" she asked hoarsely.

"It will always hurt around the level of injury, but after awhile it won't be as bad as this. That's what they say."

Kelly covered his hand with hers, noting how he inched it away so she didn't feel his weak response. "You'll do lots of things, Scott. I know you will. You have to think positively. You're tough."

"Oh, yeah, sure. A regular Superman. I don't think your 'positive thinking' attitude works for everything, Kelly. The first thing I've gotta do is either get out of this ridiculous bed or find some way to kill myself."

The impact of what he said stunned Kelly, though she didn't want him to know it. "You've got to believe in miracles."

"Ha-ha. It's going to take one to get me out of here. Otherwise, the only sport you'll find me playing is wheelchair basketball."

"Scott . . . " Kelly's voice climbed over the knot in her throat. "I love you."

"Don't. Don't love me, you idiot. It's a big mistake."

A nurse entered the room. Kelly couldn't help thinking that if the atmosphere were visible, you could have cut it with a knife at that moment. Scott glared at her, and she dropped her gaze to the expanse of white sheet. She wanted to kiss him, to reach out and run her fingers through his tangled hair.

"Time for your medication," the nurse, named Sally, said with a smile. Her words were so normal and steadying that Kelly relaxed for a split second.

"Go, Kelly," Scott ordered.

"I'll be back later," she said, trying to ignore what he said but quickly turning her back on him so that he couldn't see her tears.

When at last she drove into the circular driveway of her house, it seemed like ages since she'd been home, though it was only since that morning.

The house was California ranch-style, painted brick-red. Steps leading to the front door were bordered by pebbled flowerbeds. The lawn had a manicured, impeccable look, thanks to the gardener.

That was one thing about Kelly's father — he hired people to do a lot of jobs for him because his work was so demanding he didn't have time for the house. Kelly thought the yard had an impersonal appearance, and the house would have had it, too, if not for her and her mother. She liked stacks of magazines and knickknacks left around, and her dad had certainly collected enough mementos from the international stories he'd worked on over the years. Bird statues from Oaxaca, a Persian rug from the Mideast, dolls from different countries — the one item Kelly loved to collect. She was glad he'd taken the job on the small town newspaper so he could be home more, but she did miss the trips and the interesting stuff he brought back.

"The place is beginning to look like a curio shop," her father teased her as he came in the door.

"It's better than Early Hotel Room, Dad. I half expect to find a Gideon Bible in the drawer by your bedside."

"I just don't have time for frills," he said, setting his briefcase next to a wilting fern. "By the way, what's wrong with this plant?"

"It needs attention." Kelly giggled. "Maybe a little water."

"I once interviewed a guy who talked to his plants."

Kelly went upstairs and changed into her swimsuit. It wasn't time for school to be out, and she wanted more than anything to talk to Marilee. The neighborhood was as quiet as a tomb with everyone still in school as she slipped out to the backyard and dove into the pear-shaped swimming pool.

Kelly found herself acutely aware of her body, of its fluid, swift movements; the way she scissor-kicked, causing a gentle ruffle of a wake behind her as she swam a lap; how her arm strokes left wings on the surface, ripples spreading outward across the glassy expanse. How graceful, how perfectly in control of every limb . . . she had power over herself . . . a power that Scott no longer possessed.

They were equally strong swimmers, though his freestyle was better than hers and her breaststroke better than his. They were both prize-winning swimmers. Kelly thought of Scott's powerful legs and arms chopping through the water, and how he played tennis, dancing across the court, surprising his opponent by seeming to be in two places at once. She remembered how envious she'd been of his style, wishing she had what he had, not realizing until they talked that he was envious of hers — a style she didn't know she possessed. What it evolved into, in place of envy, was a mutual respect for one another's gifts and capabilities.

But that was gone now, Kelly reflected. *If Scott can't do all these things that I admire about him, even though I love him desperately, how will he take it — and how will I?*

He's not going to stay paralyzed, she told herself firmly. *He's going to get better, regain all his feeling.* She thrashed through the water, imagining his lifeless legs beneath the sheet.

She flopped onto her back and floated, so immersed in her thoughts of Scott that she didn't hear the redwood gate open.

"Yoo-hoo! Kelly!" Marilee dumped her schoolbooks on the chaise lounge and knelt by the side of the pool. "I came by to remind you about swim practice. Are you going?"

"I don't think I can. I should go back to the hospital tonight."

"C'mon. You can go after practice." Marilee held out a thick towel for her. "We need to talk."

Marilee could be extremely forceful at times. Kelly guessed that's what made her such a good director. She was not afraid to tell people what to do, and yet she did it in such a way that nobody got really pushed out of shape about it. People did what she told them and didn't think about her instructions until afterward.

"You look awful, Kelly. What happened today at the hospital?" Marilee scrutinized her carefully.

"I just got out of the pool. How do you expect me to look?" Kelly returned, slightly irritated.

"Stop being evasive. Just tell me."

"Okay, okay. You win." Kelly sighed, toweling her hair vigorously. "Scott told me not to love him, Marilee. How do you just stop loving someone when they get hurt?"

Kelly's voice broke as she looked to her friend for advice.

"He's traumatized, Kelly. Remember that."

"But he told me to go away, and I almost wanted to, because I can't stand seeing him like that. I just want him all better — but that's just a dream."

"I don't know anything about it, except that if I were in his situation, I would probably wonder if anyone was ever going to love me again and if I could ever walk, let alone play sports. And you know how important sports are to Scott."

"More important than anything, which is the same way I feel," Kelly said.

"Just keep him company. That's really all you can do, I guess." Marilee shrugged, not knowing what to do about this any more than Kelly did.

"Everybody at school is pulling for Scott, you know."

"He's received tons of get-well cards. I wonder if people realize just how *well* he's expected to get."

Six

"I won't eat this! It tastes like pig slop, and it's just too much work to eat!"

Scott used his good arm to upset his food tray, sending it crashing to the floor. Peach custard, pork chops, broccoli, and apple sauce merged together into a multicolored blob.

"Scott, we know you're angry," Odette Springer, his nurse, observed coolly. "I know you're feeling rotten, and I'll get you another dinner. There's sauerkraut —"

"I don't want any of it!" he screamed, his voice tearing out of his throat as if it belonged to someone else.

Odette hurried out, and an orderly came in to clean up the mess.

"Get out! Just get out!" Scott yelled, not

recognizing himself. He had never been one to lose his temper easily. But this situation twisted Scott into a different person — he wasn't sure he knew *who* he was anymore.

Will I ever return to myself? he wondered. *Everyone around here talks about 'return of function' — well, what about normal thinking? Do you lose that along with other sensations, as well? Of course,* Scott thought, *there is a specialist for everything, someone to teach you how to hold a spoon and someone to make you wiggle your toes daily. After this episode, they'll probably send in a shrink,* he guessed wryly.

At first — he realized this now — he had denied that this was really happening to him. It couldn't be as bad as all that. But it was a horrifying reality. And regardless of what the doctors, therapists, social workers, and everybody else thought they could do for him, it wasn't enough. They couldn't give him back what he wanted, and as a result, anger ran a deep, ugly route inside him that tore away more of his old self every day. He couldn't stop it. His whole reason for living was turned upside down.

Sports were useless to him. They were more a tease than a pleasure. He even hated to watch games on TV. Everything he treasured was threatened, even to the extent that as a result of having spent so many hours in the sun, his immobilized body now suffered a calcium imbalance in addition to his other problems.

Worst of all was feeling so lousy, suffering awful pain. Scott had rarely been sick a day in his life, and now he was sick of being alive, sick of not breathing properly, sick of therapists, doctors, nurses, medications. He was also sick of looking at everything from the unnatural angles that the Stryker frame afforded him.

"You should be in it for about six weeks," Dr. Nathan told him, smiling as if that was supposed to be great.

Six weeks in jail, he might as well have said.

Scott now knew the true meaning of helpless. He was it. A helpless cripple. Another question had haunted him. "Will I ever be able to have children?" he asked Dr. Nathan.

"It's very possible that you will, with your type of injury," the doctor assured him.

He and Kelly had talked about getting married someday and having kids. Now he couldn't even be sure of that.

Seeing Kelly, he knew the distance between them would broaden, until they separated. He could see it coming, and he wanted to be armed against it, as if that might alleviate the pain. He would never be a challenge to her again. Her long brown legs, running away from him — *She said she loves me but she loves what I was, not what I've become. No one can love what I've become.*

"Will you eat more?" The nurse was there with the tray, not daring to bring it anywhere near the bed.

"No. Take it away, please." Scott wanted to hide under the covers and pretend this whole scene had never occurred.

Later, Odette Springer came back to take Scott to therapy. While his muscles were being worked, the therapist, Jackie Oliviera, chatted encouragingly about his progress.

"You're responding very well. Can't you see how much better your grasp is already? Your feet are coming along, too."

"How soon will I walk?"

"That's a long way off, Scott. But you're doing beautifully."

He suspected they were making it up. They always avoided committing themselves, so that he wasn't sure when to believe them.

In the corner was a woman Scott had never seen before. Her name tag identified her as Dr. Elene Rodriguez, Psychologist. Maybe he needed one right now. He was going pretty bananas.

"Your girlfriend is very sweet," Jackie said as she turned the frame.

A bitter taste filled Scott's mouth. "Yeah.

She is, but I don't want to see her until I'm better."

Jackie shot him a sharp look, but it wasn't a remark she hadn't heard before.

"That's no way to talk. She seems crazy about you," she offered.

She went about her business, not saying more, unable to help wondering how these two young people would manage, knowing all too well how rocky the road was for couples dealing with an accident such as this.

"Hi, Kelly. How're you doing? We heard about Scott," Deanna Brasile said, then proceeded to blow a huge bubble with her gum, snapping it loudly between her teeth. Deanna was petite with short, curly hair and a vivacious personality.

Kelly felt oddly conspicuous in the crowded hallway of Clancy High. A few kids she knew walked by, staring at her as if she were somehow different. Next to Deanna stood her boyfriend, Mason Belinsky, and Chloe Barnes with Reggie Holiday, all friends of hers and Scott's.

"Geez, it's awful," Chloe breathed, tugging on a leg warmer, which she insisted on wearing over jeans.

"He's making progress, though, Chloe," Kelly said hopefully, wanting to make the prognosis sound good.

"What exactly happened, do you know? Darren told me he was in a surfing accident."

"And now he's paralyzed. . . . Will it go away?"

"He's paralyzed from the middle of his chest down, and he has some use of his arms and hands right now, but that's supposed to come back. He may walk again, but it won't be for a while." Kelly wondered what they pictured when she told them that. It was so hard to visualize Scott as any other way but completely active.

"Poor guy. What's that gonna do to his life?" Mason wagged his head in dismay.

"I think that's what Scott's wondering right now, too." Kelly smiled. "But he's a fighter. He'll manage just fine."

"Yeah, sure."

"I'd like to see him," said Reggie.

"Why don't you call him, Reggie? Then he can tell you if he wants to see you or not."

"Hey, we missed you at swimming practice, Horn! What's up?"

Kelly turned around and explained to Marta Baker what had happened.

"What's this gonna do to you? It's too bad, I know, but the coach is concerned. And Sledgewick's having a fit — you haven't shown for three tennis practices, either."

"I don't know. I want to stay with the team, Marta, you know that. But I'm not sure if I can keep up with everything and Scott. . . . "

"Let the doctors take care of him, Kelly," Marta said, shaking her head. "You can't do anything for him right now, can you?"

Kelly was scared about the teams. She didn't want to forfeit the progress she'd made so far this year, but already it seemed nearly impossible to meet all these obligations. Perhaps it would all straighten itself out, she hoped. Perhaps Scott would be moved closer so it would be easier to see him. Her problems seemed so slight in comparison with his.

Kelly excused herself to go to class, clutching her books in a white-knuckled grasp. It was the first day she had been able to face school since the accident, and although she understood everyone's curiosity and concern, she felt weird. It was a strain on her to have to explain repeatedly what was wrong with Scott, knowing that they couldn't really grasp the immensity of it, as she hadn't been able to. There were so many problems for Scott to deal with that her friends would never know about, but Kelly was fast educating herself on spinal cord injury.

Sitting in biology, watching Sallie Mattison and Kurt Widenauer surreptitiously passing love notes back and forth while Mr. Addams droned endlessly on about single-celled organisms, Kelly yearned for the normalness of that kind of exchange — the kind of goofy thing she and Scott would do — if Scott were here.

She glanced over at Scott's seat four rows away, where he'd been moved just before the accident, because he and Kelly kept horsing around so much in class. The empty space gave Kelly a start.

She had hoped she could forget about him a little in school, but the empty desk reminded her. And on the hockey field as she strapped on her shin guards, she could hear Scott call across the fence — "Strap 'em tight, and don't forget the metal spikes!"

Then he'd dance back onto the tennis court, which was adjacent to the field, his image slightly altered by the cyclone fence that separated them. She stood for a moment, remembering his slender, muscular back rippling beneath a white cotton T-shirt, his laughter trembling on the air.

"Hey, Horn, are you playing?"

Deanna, playing goalie, rudely interrupted her thoughts.

Squeezing her eyes shut, Kelly cinched the shin guard a little too tightly before answering. Then she realized everyone was patiently waiting for her.

"Yeah, I'm playing," she said, her heart

not in it as she trudged slowly over to the others, who eyed her curiously.

Marilee swiped at herself with a skimpy towel in the locker room. "Well, tennis was a complete burnout. I need you to team up with."

"Not today, Mare. I'm not the world's greatest athlete right now." Kelly stuffed her dirty gym clothes into her locker, exchanging them for a T-shirt and overalls. "After blowing two goals, my team's not too happy with me."

"Did they say anything?" Marilee frowned, her eyebrows coming together in a golden ripple.

"No. That makes it worse, really. People usually give me a bad time, and it perks me up. But not today." They exchanged glances.

"Forget about it. Things'll get back to normal, you'll see. They just don't know what to do or say, you know?" Marilee's voice was sympathetic, a balm to Kelly's seething emotions. "Let's go get an ice cream or something, and talk."

"I don't think so, Marilee. I should call Scott." She reached for her purse and was about to say good-bye, when Marilee caught her by the arm.

"Look, Kelly. This isn't easy for you, but stop feeling guilty because you're okay and

58

because you've got the use of your body. You're not helping Scott by being a sad sack." Kelly scrunched up her mouth, ready to cry. "C'mon, I'm buying."

What started out to be a simple ice cream outing stretched into an afternoon, as Ben Forester, editor of the school newspaper, *The Triumph*, buttonholed Kelly, bought her a soda, and chatted for a while, asking about Scott.

"You'll have to talk to Scott yourself, Ben. I don't know if he wants you to do a story on him. He's in a state of shock right now," she explained. "Maybe in a couple of weeks, he might consider it."

"I'll call him, Kelly. It might cheer him up." His gold-brown eyes studied her with an interest Kelly found oddly disconcerting. "And, meanwhile, how are you doing?"

She smiled. "Trying to stay normal, I guess. Helping Scott get adjusted."

"Well, he ought to do real well with someone like you to keep him afloat." Ben grinned, and she was aware of what a nice face he had. Friendly, and he was probably not at all aware of the impact of what he'd just said and how Kelly connected it with the accident.

Everything hurt. Everywhere she turned, there was something to burn and tease and jolt. She felt like a lump of raw emotion, ready to burst into a million pieces at a moment's notice.

When Kelly and Marilee arrived at Kelly's house, her father said there had been a call from Mrs. Martin.

"Scott contracted an infection and his blood pressure is unstable. He's angry, which the doctors say is a good sign, but of course, the infection and blood pressure present problems."

"I'm going over there, Dad." Kelly dumped her books on the table in the hallway.

"I'll go with you, Kelly," Marilee offered.

"No, I want to go by myself. Will everyone just leave me alone?"

"Not unless you calm down," her father admonished sternly. "Now, if you don't get hold of yourself, you'll go barging into that room, upsetting Scott more than he already is, and possibly making things worse. His family is probably already driving him nuts, as you can imagine the Martins doing, the way they disagree. So keep your cool. Maybe it would be a good idea for Marilee or me to drive you over there."

Kelly was shaking from head to toe. Her father and Marilee put their arms around her, nearly suffocating her.

"You're both going to make me cry more. Now cut it out," she told them, tears wetting her face.

$S\underline{even}$

The hallway seemed dark and cold to Kelly as she walked along the ward, her footsteps echoing hollowly on the freshly waxed linoleum. An astringent scent mingled with the aroma of dinner presented an unappetizing combination, which she wondered if the patients noticed.

Dr. Nathan and Mrs. Martin greeted her outside Scott's room.

"It's not unusual for anyone who's spent two weeks in bed, even without a spinal cord injury, to experience low blood pressure," Dr. Nathan explained. "But he's apparently contracted an infection, which has elevated the blood pressure and which we'll have to watch carefully."

"Is he going to be okay, though? This won't make it any worse?"

'It' meaning the paralysis, Kelly surmised, listening to Mrs. Martin's question.

"No, it won't get worse, unless his blood pressure goes up too high."

Mrs. Martin buried her mouth in a handkerchief, her eyes misting over.

"We have him sedated right now, and he's resting comfortably. I don't think there's any need for worry at this point."

Kelly was getting anxious to see Scott, and by the time she went in she had mentally composed what she would say to him. It was difficult to have a conversation, she found, with someone who hadn't moved much since the last time you saw him. Her life was full of many activities, where his was a constant struggle just to make it through a daily, rigorous routine.

"Feeling better?" She pretended to smooth the covers.

"Look at these legs." He thumped his limbs dramatically. "They just tremble whenever they want to, and I can't do anything about it. And worse, I can't feel them."

"You will. Everyone says you will, with therapy."

Scott looked her full in the face, his own flushed pink over a fading tan. "Do you want someone you have to push around in a wheel-chair? I hope I make it to wheels eventually."

"It doesn't matter, Scott. I love you." Kelly's throat ached, but she dared not cry in front of him.

"It does matter, and you'd better pay attention to it. You can't pretend it doesn't matter, because it will. You're not thinking of the future, our future. You're only dreaming this romantic dream of us together — most likely running or walking together — which is total garbage."

"Scott —"

"No, listen to me. I'm really angry this happened to me, not just because of me, but because I had plans for *us,* and now they're washed up. I can't live up to your expectations or even my own. All that's happening to me are problems, and they're all tough. They may look easy to you, but they're not."

"I know they're not." Kelly trembled. She reached out to put her arms around Scott, but he withdrew.

"Don't touch me, Kelly. You don't want me."

"Please, Scott, give me a chance."

"No. I don't want you ever feeling responsible for me or pitying me. I want you to get out of my life, understand? I think it's the only way."

"No. I still think we've got a lot to give each other."

"Have you seen how I eat? It's funny to watch."

"You'll learn to do it yourself and become an expert," she said knowingly.

"I'll always need help, Kelly. That's what I hate. I want to be able to do everything for myself."

"Aren't you wanting the impossible?"

"Sure. Look at all I did before the accident. When I was normal. I just bet your days aren't as boring as mine are right now." He stared hard at her, a cold stare that chilled her to the bone.

"What did you do today, anyway? Just as an example."

"Played hockey at school, took a science test, and went to an ice-cream parlor."

"See? You call that boring? It's everyday to you, but to me, it's only a dream."

A surge of hot guilt overtook Kelly. She changed the subject. "Ben Forester wants to talk to you, by the way."

"I don't want to talk to anyone. I want to be left alone." His mouth drooped into a bitter line. "I want you to go away and not come back. Find somebody who can walk. You don't need me for a boyfriend."

Flames climbed her cheeks. "Do you really mean that?"

"Yes."

Kelly remembered that she'd better not upset him, so she left quickly, muttering a choked good-bye and feeling glad to get away from him.

E^{ight}

The next day Kelly and her father went to school to talk to her coach.

"I've had phone calls from two coaches today, and it's nothing to do with the paper," Kelly's father said, frowning, as they drove to the high school. He knew many high school coaches, as they often made submissions to the sports page. "I'm not trying to put pressure on you, Kelly, but you've got to decide whether you're going to put energy into these sports or if you're going to relinquish what you've gained this year. You've got a good record and it's a shame to spoil it."

"So much has happened, Dad. I can't decide what to do. Maybe I should give up something."

"Give up? That doesn't sound like you."

"How am I supposed to handle all this?"

"Just do it. You can arrange seeing Scott so you don't miss practice. You have to start thinking about how this is going to affect your future."

They walked into Sledgewick's office, tripping over a mound of tennis shoes that held the door open. The wall behind the coach was covered with ribbons and photos and competition announcements.

Sledgewick was a burly man in black shorts and a white T-shirt, which Kelly guessed was his uniform since she rarely saw him in anything else. The one time she'd seen him in a suit, he looked so uncomfortable she didn't recognize him.

"Well, it looks to me like I lost not only one tennis player, but two, this season," the coach began.

Kelly explained about Scott being moved to the Spinal Cord Unit and how difficult it had been to juggle her life since.

"Yeah, I know that, Kelly. But maybe this is your big test. D'you really think Scott would like to see you give up everything on account of his injury? I mean, you can drop tennis if you really think it's too much for you, but I'm asking you to stay. We can use you on the team. You've got good endurance and a backhand that won't quit."

"I can't replace Scott."

"So what? We're not looking for a replacement for Scott. We just need good players, and you're one of them. There are some things you do better than him."

"Like what?" Kelly was curious.

"Like, you're springier and faster than him. You can be in two places at once, and he can't. He's too big a boy." Sledgewick leaned back in his chair, tapping it against the wall. "You can live with that, can't you?" The coach always addressed a player's competitive spirit.

"Look, I'll try, Mr. Sledgewick. That's all I can do."

"That's the spirit." He took Kelly's father aside. "Mickey, take care of that girl. Don't let her slip. She's got too much going for her."

"I'm doing my best. She's stubborn, and devoted to Scott. And we just don't know how he's going to fare, either."

"Yeah, it's tough. I feel for you, all of you."

"It sounds like he needs you more now than ever," Kelly's mother told her over the phone that night. "He probably doesn't mean what he's saying."

"Mom, he's really depressed. I'm so worried about him. I mean, in a way, he's right. I haven't been facing what kind of life we would have together . . . if that's how we end up. We just sort of figured before this happened that we'd stay together, planning to go to the same college even. What should I do, Mom? Stay away from him or keep showing up at the hospital? I can't say I feel exactly wanted."

"I can imagine. Ask someone professional, Kelly. They know how to handle these cases. I'm sure there's a psychologist affiliated with the hospital who can help you with this problem. Maybe Mrs. Martin is seeing someone right now."

"She looks like a stick figure."

"I would, too, if this happened to you. Poor woman. It's terrible for her." She sighed. Kelly heard her turn down the radio, then she said, "Hey, I'd like to get out there to be with you. Maybe a visit from your mother might help?"

"D'you mean that?"

"Yeah. I can always get away to come to California for a few days for you, darling. And it would be good for both of us, don't you think? We can talk for hours."

"I'd love it. I feel better already."

"I'll make plans, then. Later."

"Our culture, or Western culture in general, is a very body-oriented society, whether it be in physical fitness, or prowess, or beauty," Dr. Rodriguez, the psychologist, told

Kelly. She was an attractive, dark-haired woman in her thirties, with a manner that made Kelly feel very much at ease. "And when a person experiences a loss of body function such as Scott has, this causes him to lose his perception of himself in society."

"That sounds like Scott. He's an athlete, planning to make a career in sports."

"Then this accident is even more difficult for him. People who express themselves physically have the hardest time. But he has to go through these phases of psychological trauma. Some people call it the 'grief cycle.' It's a process of adjustment that includes denial, shock, depression, anger, and finally, acceptance. The family also goes through it to a certain degree, so it's very important for everyone to be educated so they know what to expect."

"How can we help Scott if he refuses to see us? I mean, me." Kelly averted her eyes to the floor. "He doesn't want to see me anymore. That really hurts. I just want to be close to him, be supportive. D'you know what I mean?"

"Sure, but remember that to him, you represent what he used to be. He doesn't understand that you still want him and love him. He can't believe it because he's so changed. The reality of his disability has snuck in, and he knows he's got a lot of work ahead of him, so much work that most of the time he's thinking he'll never make it and what's the use? He needs to know he can have a life that can be productive and full. He needs to see other people making it, which he'll see in rehab. He feels like a burden to you and everybody else. He's angry, which is a good sign. It's better to show anger than to hold it all in and withdraw."

"I just hope he gets over it," Kelly said. "I don't know how *I* feel anymore. We were so close, and suddenly, I can't get near him, can't touch him. He's almost like a stranger to me. And it's not because of his body. So what do I do now? Do I keep coming around . . . force myself on him?"

"He's got to know you're still in his life and that you care. Even if your romance tapers off, you should maintain the friendship, if you can." Dr. Rodriguez studied Kelly, as if gauging how much she cared for Scott.

Kelly squirmed under her scrutiny. "Scott and I love each other . . . or at least, I know I still love him. Whether or not it's still mutual, I don't know."

"He's got to fight other battles right now, Kelly. He doesn't have the energy to fight for your love as well. It takes a lot of courage to do just what he's doing at the moment, although his progress might look insubstantial from your point of view. The best you can do is be there for him. Don't force yourself on him — just make sure he knows your love is there."

Kelly felt guilty for doubting Scott, for worrying over his reactions to her. Wouldn't she feel unlovable in his position? Wouldn't she experience all those same doubts and fears he was experiencing right now?

She came away from Dr. Rodriguez's office questioning herself. Was there a limit to her love? Did she really think she and Scott would get through this and stay together?

Kelly honestly didn't know. The Scott she once knew and loved had turned cold eyes upon her, curling inward to feed on his anger in a place she couldn't reach. Maybe this was how he should be, but it wasn't how she wanted him.

Nothing was right. The psychologist's words had simply kicked up a whole flutter of doubts in Kelly's mind. Kelly could not believe that she was even beginning to question her love for Scott, which now seemed as tenuous as a spider's thread stretched between them.

N<u>ine</u>

Regina Horn possessed the same sleek, crow-black hair as her daughter, curving gently against her cheek and accentuating her wide, brown eyes. Kelly could hardly contain her joy as her mother stepped self-assuredly into the airline terminal at San Francisco Airport.

They fell into each other's arms, Kelly holding on a beat longer than usual, savoring the warmth and scent of her mother, which she'd missed more than she thought.

"You look taller," Regina said, holding her at arm's length to study her more carefully.

"It's the heels, Mom." Kelly giggled, noticing that she and her mother were nearly the same height.

Regina's maroon tweed suit fit her willowy frame perfectly. Clothes always looked as though they were tailored especially for her, and she owned so many now, Kelly couldn't remember seeing her in anything twice.

"You also look tired, darling. It's been rough on you, hasn't it?" Her mother's sympathy tripped Kelly's tears.

"Oh, it's only been awful, Mom. I don't know how I can describe it to you." She buried her face in her mother's shoulder, feeling all her maturity fall away. How small and babyish she felt, but there was no stopping the flood that darkened the tweed suit.

"Come on. Let's get my bags and get out of here. We've got so much to talk about."

Regina marshalled her out of the choked waiting area and down to the baggage room, where a heavy-set man handled the suitcases like the gorilla in the Samsonite commerical.

At home, as Regina unpacked, Kelly watched admiringly as her mother littered her belongings across the bed.

"One of the things your father dislikes about me, Kelly, is my ability to spread clothes from one end of a room to another."

"Well, he still has to live with that trait." Kelly laughed. "I do the same thing."

Regina's clothes were matched for traveling, and it looked like this time she was working with maroon — everything revolving around two suits. "I probably won't need any of this for this visit," she observed ruefully. "This is the suitcase I always keep packed, just in case of an emergency. It's silly, but I'm not comfortable away from you and your father."

"I wish I could escape with you. I'm ready to steal away in the baggage compartment right now," Kelly said, folding a bright red scarf and sliding it into one of the cedar-scented drawers.

"You know, if you want to escape, Kelly, you can come to New York anytime and stay for a short visit."

"I know, but I have the swim team and the tennis team. . . ." *And all these problems,* she felt like adding, but instead she said, "But it does sound tempting."

The Horns ate at a popular restaurant in San Francisco, Tadishe's Grill. The lively atmosphere lifted Kelly and she was almost her old self again. Waiters teased her, her mother laughed, her father told jokes, and Kelly enjoyed herself thoroughly. She hadn't realized what she had been missing the past couple of months — being out in the world with active people. At school she was sort of half there, a dreamer passing through her days. Her world had been shaved down to the hospital walls, and her focus was there also.

"You're not eating much, Kelly." Regina frowned at her with concern.

"Dad keeps complaining about that, too. You'd think he'd be glad the food bill's so small."

"Don't joke about it. You shouldn't let yourself get so down that you don't eat." Her mother studied her wan face. "Are you feeling guilty for having fun? Is that it?"

"Sort of. I keep thinking it will be a long time before Scott can do this, and the way he's acting, I wonder if he'll want to."

"Oh, come on. He'll adapt."

Kelly related what the psychologist had told her.

"I think I know just what you need," Regina stated with a mysterious smile. "There's this little place your father and I used to go to...."

"I don't feel like mingling, Mom," Kelly declined.

Regina pulled her out of her seat, like Marilee might've done. "You may not feel like it now, but I can see who needs some instant therapy."

There was no arguing with her mother once she'd made up her mind to do something. She marched Kelly and her father out of the restaurant, oblivious to the admiring stares that followed her.

Kelly's mother looked like one of Kelly's

contemporaries in her svelte designer jeans and silk shirt. At Dave's Disco, whose clientele was generally under twenty-five, Regina caused a few heads to turn. Mickey Horn looked only slightly out of place, but soon caught the spirit of the setting.

A strobe light fluttered across the mass of dancers. One lone purple spotlight was trained on the lead singer, a boy of about eighteen, with punk, blond hair and a bright purple shirt with green pants. The rhythm guitarist had the same reddish-brown hair as Scott, and when the strobe picked him out, Kelly thought she saw Scott's smile.

"Would you like to dance?"

Regina nudged her daughter, and Kelly looked up to find Ben Forester waiting expectantly for her reply.

"What're you doing here?" she cried in surprise.

"It's one of my favorite hangouts," he said, grinning widely. "You didn't answer my question."

"Oh, sure. I'd love to."

She folded into his arms easily. The image of her and Scott dancing together came to mind but was quickly replaced by a picture of Scott as he was at that moment, trapped.

"I haven't seen you around much. Where've you been?"

"I guess Scott takes up a lot of my time," Kelly said. "And swimming."

"I called Scott, but he doesn't want to talk to me."

"I know. He's going through a rough time right now. I wish there was something I could do for him." The pressure of Ben's hand against the small of her back felt nice, and his breath lifting her hair shot warm sensations along her neck.

"I'm sure you're doing a lot. Just being there — your smiling face will make him want to get better."

"I think my face makes him mad right now, Ben. Like a red rag to a bull."

"Maybe he's thinking about all the guys who would like to take you out. Did you ever consider that?"

Kelly met his gaze, wondering briefly if Ben was one of those guys, for she hadn't seen anyone else noticing her. "No," she replied uncertainly. "Scott and I are really close."

"Hey, don't get defensive, Kelly. I'm only stating a fact. Guys are interested in you. You're a great person. Look around." His dimples deepened when he smiled.

Her fingers felt hot and liquid in Ben's, and she disengaged them quickly, as if they were on fire. She thought only Scott did that to her.

"You have to start having some fun, too, you know, Kelly. You can't hide from the world. Scott will get well."

"Who says I'm hiding? And anyway, you don't realize how hard it's going to be for him to get better. It's all uphill."

"Hard work doesn't stop somebody like him. He's a winner."

Kelly smiled. She couldn't dislike Ben for being honest, could she? And he was sweet, warming her.

"Thanks for the dance," she said, drawing away.

"How about another?" His eyes held hers.

In spite of herself and of her mother's amused glances, Kelly agreed. They danced for a long time, fast and slow. She finally relaxed, allowing her worries and confusion to be scattered by the lights and music.

Her parents were dancing, too. It always amazed Kelly how her mother could make everyone feel perfectly comfortable in the weirdest situations.

"How's the swimming and tennis going? Have you been keeping up?" Ben broke into her thoughts, his breath on her ear, sending shivers down her spine.

"I'm trying to, though I'm falling behind in tennis. We have relays coming up. Ugh, don't remind me — it gets me nervous."

"I notice Jan Graham's coming along with the butterfly. That's one hard stroke."

"Yeah, she's good. Do you watch practice?"

"Oh, once in awhile. I pick up my little sister, Barbie, on Tuesdays."

All too soon, the evening was over. Reluctantly, Kelly said good-bye.

"Can I call you?" Ben wanted to know.

"I guess so," she replied, guilt returning.

"That was good for you," Regina insisted as they walked to the car. "You need to keep your spirits up, and a little attention never hurt anyone."

"I hope you're right," Kelly said, but she knew by the pleasant flame fluttering inside her that it could do real harm.

"Swimming's good therapy for the disabled, Scott." Mr. Malmin was making his biweekly visit to see Scott, armed with several old issues of *Sports Illustrated* and a spiel on getting out there and getting involved.

"I'm not dying to get back on the swim team, Mr. Malmin. I mean, everybody's just crazy to have someone like me on their side, right? Why don't you consider me for the mascot position instead?"

Scott felt critical, abrasive — everything anyone said rubbed him the wrong way. Why did they have to keep coming around with their good ideas and suggestions, when all he wanted to do was attempt to disappear?

"Scott, you're not helping yourself, d'you know that? All I want is to let you know there are possibilities out there for you, after you get finished with rehab, or maybe it can be a part of your rehabilitation. Who knows? But you do have a future."

"Let's just get the gimp moving again, then we'll toss him in the pool and let him fend for himself, right?"

"Scott . . ."

Scott laughed coldly. "Hey, why not? I've got nothing else to lose — it's all gone."

"You have a lot . . . your family . . . Kelly."

"I don't want Kelly coming around anymore." He said it abruptly, instantly sorry he'd confided in his coach. But lately, words popped out of his mouth unbidden, things he'd just as soon keep quiet about.

"You shouldn't send her away. She needs you, too. I notice her mind's not on her swimming these days, and I'm always after her. She's missed a few practices, too."

Scott suddenly grew quiet. "She shouldn't do that."

"No. We've got relays coming up soon."

Life, as molasses-slow as it appeared to him, was passing him by on the outside. "Who's swimming freestyle?"

"Richard Dixon and Mark Hunt."

"Good."

"We're really missing you, kid. You know that, don't you?"

"Yeah, sure. But there'll be others." Suddenly, Scott wished the coach would just bug off and leave him alone. It was too painful remembering past successes — glories that would never be his again. Was he doomed to be a regretful has-been athlete, wheeling himself to meets?

"You can still be a good teacher and coach, Scott. Do you think that because you've been hurt people are going to forget you exist?"

"Something like that. It already happens when people who don't work around here see me in a chair. I'm sort of ignored."

There were many things he couldn't explain to Mr. Malmin, who had never experienced the futility, the acute helplessness, that would always be a part of Scott's life. He was supposed to get used to it, overcome whatever barriers he could and go on, but he didn't think he ever would. All his life he'd been a strong kid, and strength never made room for helplessness in any form.

In the back of his mind, Scott knew he'd have to get up on his feet and get as far away from helplessness as he could. He had to be strong again.

* * *

"Pay attention, Horn! You're supposed to hit the ball, not the net!"

Kelly cringed at Sledgewick's bellowing. He was like a bull circling the tennis court, huffing and puffing at her with every move she made. Her confidence was waning daily with his onslaughts, her grip on her racket becoming weak and clumsy.

"What's wrong, Kelly? You don't seem your old self at all," Marta Baker whispered to her.

"Too much is going on," she mumbled in reply before the ball came hurtling at her. *Whap!* Whew, she got it over the net.

"It's about time, Horn! Now let's see your serve!"

Kelly gulped cold air. Marta gave her the high sign and she nodded back, hoping for enough skill to do this right in front of the coach. She couldn't blame him for being impatient with her. She was beginning to get tired of herself, too. She'd always been a good tennis player, and now she was downright awful.

Whap! Into the net.

"Try again." Sledgewick's annoyance bubbled close to the surface. All eyes were pinned on Kelly.

Whap! Another ball into the net.

"One more and you're out."

Kelly glowered, hit the ball, and luckily it

sailed over the net. Deanna smashed it back, causing Marta to buckle as she ran for it and missed.

"What a relief, Horn! I was beginning to think you were only good for net balls." Sledgewick watched her carefully for the rest of the period, which lasted five minutes longer, and then he called her over.

"Kelly, I can't have you playing in this condition. And I don't want to take you off the team — you're too good. But I'm going to have to bench you for the tourney."

Kelly felt tears start to gather and bit them back. "Yeah, okay. I guess there isn't much I can say, because I know you have to do it, and I can't guarantee I'll be any better than I am right now."

"Well, I know you'll be back in full form when this . . . is over. It's just a matter of time." He slapped her shoulder. "Take it easy, kid. And don't stop coming to practice. I like your face."

She managed to smile. Marta fell in beside her as they trudged to the gym. "What was that all about?"

"I'm benched for the tourney."

"Oh, no. What're you gonna do?"

"Just what I said. I'll sit and watch you guys play. I'm lucky Sledge still wants me on the team. You know how lousy I've been lately, and I can't snap out of it."

"I'm sorry."

"So am I, but that's the breaks."

"You're being awfully brave. How's swimming?"

"So-so, but I'll get through the next meet."

"What're you going to do . . . about Scott, I mean?"

She shrugged. "Just stick around and try to make him feel better."

"You must be getting good at that."

"Yeah. Nurse Horn here." They laughed, but Kelly felt lousy. She'd lost something on account of Scott, but she also felt guilty for worrying about a trivial tennis game. After all, it was small in comparison with Scott's loss. At least she would have a chance to play tennis again.

Ten

People at school didn't ask about Scott very much anymore. Kelly's dad said that was not unusual since the accident was no longer "front page news," as he put it. Two months after the accident, students probably figured he was well on his way to recovery by now or had forgotten about him entirely.

Kelly thought some kids were avoiding her. Of course, not Marilee or Chloe, people close to her, but some of the swim team that she used to clown around with when Scott was still part of the group. She found herself standing sharply alone at the edge of the pool at practice while the others yakked about dates, sports, and school, and she longed to be included.

Marilee suggested that perhaps it was because she wasn't dating like everyone else. "I mean, let's face it, Kelly, you don't have anything trivial to blab about."

Kelly got defensive. "Sure I do! They're just not asking me, that's all!"

"Well, I hate to tell you this, but you're not as much fun as you used to be, Kelly. And for a good reason; nobody blames you, I'm sure. It's just that people don't like to hang around somebody who's always looking miserable. They don't even want to walk up and say hi!"

"I'm not like that, am I?" Even as she asked the question, Kelly remembered her mom urging her to smile, look like she was having a good time, even if she wasn't.

"Yeah, I'm afraid so. Scott is becoming a big drain on you. It's really noticeable because you've always been such a happy person, Kelly. What're you going to do if he doesn't walk again? Have you thought about that?"

Kelly was fuming. "What do you mean? Of course, I've thought about nothing else since the accident! And he *will* walk again. And anyway, just because Scott's paralyzed, it doesn't mean we can't love each other anymore!"

"Yes, but how much does being paralyzed change your love? Did you think of that?"

"Marilee, leave me alone! Love doesn't change because of physical changes!" Kelly felt shaky and unsure about that. Even she had to admit there was a terrific strain on the relationship.

"You can't ignore it. It bothers you and it bothers Scott. He's letting you go, he's giving you an out. So consider it. Remember, you told me you had a great time with Ben."

"I shouldn't have told you about that."

"Well, don't feel guilty, for goodness' sake." She grinned. "Friends are to share secrets with. And Ben is a juicy secret — one you could enjoy more."

"I don't want to. You don't understand, Marilee. Nobody's going through what Scott and I are going through right now. I can't just forget Scott and go off with Ben. I just can't."

"Somebody has gone through just what you're going through, Kelly. You should get in touch with people who are in the same position."

"Maybe that's not such a bad idea," Kelly considered, knowing that she had to try everything. She couldn't imagine life without Scott, but at the same time, she was not imagining a life with him, either.

"Kelly, I have this terrific idea. Why don't you come to Chloe's slumber party?" suggested Marilee.

"I didn't know about it."

"Well, it's tomorrow night. She didn't ask you because we figured you wouldn't come, but you've got to. You're becoming a hermit."

"Gee, thanks." But Kelly knew she was right.

Chloe's house was a two-story clapboard, reminiscent of a New England farmhouse, which Marilee loved because she was from Connecticut.

"All it needs is a few inches of snow around it and it will be a dream come true."

"And to be transported three thousand miles," giggled Chloe, a dark-haired beauty with pert features and thick, Elizabeth Taylor eyelashes that needed no mascara.

Lana Biddle had brought some delicious butterscotch brownies; Kelly and Marilee had made their specialty, Tollhouse cookies; and Nancy Erlich brought something organic, as usual — a mixture of tofu and carrots that was enough to make any dentist smile (her father was a dentist). Wendy Jossi made cupcakes, Deanna brought chips and dips, and Marta brought some sausage rolls made by her brother, since she usually burned everything she tried to cook.

Chloe's bedroom was a converted family room, and it accommodated eight girls easily. It was decorated in plum and pink, with one whole corner devoted to trophies won in track and tennis, and the envy of everyone was the wall-length walk-in closet that housed about a dozen warm-up suits, in addition to regular clothes, and more running and tennis shoes than Kelly had ever seen in one person's wardrobe.

After the girls demolished a giant pizza made by Chloe's mom, Chloe suggested they have a bike race.

"Do you have enough bikes?" Kelly wondered aloud.

Chloe's four brothers were away at college. "Sure, we've got plenty," she replied mysteriously.

She led the way out to the garage and switched on the light. A collective gasp followed, then giggles.

Lined up along the side of the garage were seven tricycles.

"You expect us to ride those?"

"Sure. Why not? You're big enough, aren't you?"

Bursts of laughter erupted as everyone picked out a trike and pushed it to the driveway. Gladys, Chloe's mom, stood outside with a cap pistol. "Okay, take care of these bikes, girls, because every kid in the neighborhood will be after you if you don't."

"Whose idea was this, Chloe?"

Chloe simply beamed. "Enjoy the race," was all she said.

"Ready, set, GO!"

Eight teenage girls on trikes hurtled down the driveway and into the deserted street. A few children peeked out their windows, probably worried about their trikes, Kelly figured with amusement. Ahead, Nancy Erlich's long legs were splayed on either side of her machine as she tried to get it going, skinning her knees in the process.

Deanna, the shortest of the group, whizzed past everyone. Chloe stuck her legs on the handlebars, grinning wildly as she careened down the street. Marilee tried pushing from the back, then jumping on at high speed. Wendy Jossi tipped over midway through the race, and Lana smashed into her from the rear, sending them both into gales of laughter.

As they rounded the curve, the contestants saw Chloe's mom at the finish line, a long pink ribbon which wrapped around Deanna's neck as she finished first.

"Congratulations, Dee! You win first prize!" Mrs. Barnes handed her a pink-wrapped package.

"I hope it's not something to eat."

Everyone giggled as they clustered around Deanna.

"C'mon, Wendy! Get a move on."

Wendy hobbled along, puffing and panting. "This is not my forte, you know."

"Wait until we tell everyone that the girl who wins the cross-country bike race can't even ride a trike."

The group doubled over in laughter and Deanna could barely open her package. She pulled back the tissue to behold a key chain with a plastic tennis shoe attached to it. "Just what I needed. Thanks!"

Mrs. Barnes laughed. "Now that you've all worked off that pizza, how about some refreshments?"

The tricyclists followed her back up the street, giggling and joking.

"Wait 'til Mason hears about this, Deanna. He's gonna die!"

"Don't tell him! He already thinks I've lost my marbles!"

"Hey, Marta, isn't that Ted?" Kelly called out, seeing the lanky boy peddling toward them on his unicycle.

"What're you doing here, Ted?" Marta asked in embarrassment.

"I came to see what you were up to. Somebody said you were having a trike race down here, and I had to see for myself. Who won?"

"Deanna."

"Congratulations." He stifled the urge to

laugh. "You realize this is fodder for the school paper?"

"Do you realize you might get your neck wrung for writing about it?" Marta threatened, and they all laughed.

"Big deal, Marta. Let him write about us. It makes us look fascinating." Marilee stuck her nose in the air dramatically. "As we are."

Ted chuckled and said good-bye.

After putting the tricycles away, the girls sat around the fire, an array of goodies spread out before them. Chloe dragged out a stack of board games and piled them on the carpet.

"Anyone for a game of Scrabble?" she shouted above the conversation.

Two of the girls quickly set up the playing pieces and half the group played Scrabble.

"It's good to see you having fun, Kelly," Chloe said. "Lately, it's been really hard to talk to you."

"You've been down in the dumps a lot," Lana said.

"I know, and I'm sorry."

"Don't be. I mean, you've got a right to be feeling how you are." Marta reflected. "I don't know what I'd do if that happened to Ted. It must sorta leave you out in left field."

"It does. I don't like to go around moping, but it's real hard to keep thinking positive when things aren't looking all that good for a long period of time."

"Scott'll get better, won't he?" Deanna asked.

"Yeah, but very slowly, and he'll never be the same as he was. He probably won't be able to play tennis or surf again, but he can do other things. It's a matter of getting him to feel hopeful about his future."

"That must be hard. How hopeful can you feel?"

"Well, you've got to figure you're still alive. You can still function, maybe not quite the same way, but in his case, he'll be able to do nearly everything he was able to do before. He's just staying miserable right now, but that's part of getting better, too."

"Really?"

"Sure. You have to go through a depression. Some people never get out of it, though, so that scares me." It was the first time Kelly had spoken so frankly in front of a group of people, and she felt a little nervous at divulging so much at once.

"I don't think most people realize what you and Scott are going through, kiddo," Marilee offered sympathetically.

"None of us realized it was going to be so tough, Kelly. You just think about the paralysis, but not all the other stuff."

"I could tell you tons of 'other stuff,' but

we'd be here all night." She chuckled. "Anyway, I want you all to know I'm having a great time tonight. This is the first time I've had a good laugh in a long time. And it feels wonderful."

"You don't feel guilty?" Chloe wanted to know.

"No. For once, I don't. Should I?" Kelly frowned with concern.

Marilee stepped in, shoving a butterscotch brownie into her friend's palm. "No, you shouldn't. You didn't cause Scott's accident, and I'm quite sure he doesn't want you to sit around being miserable because of it. Right, gang?"

"Right."

"When Sledge benched you, Kelly, I was really worried about you. It was such a shame to have to give up the tourney like that."

"It's not forever, Chloe. I'll play next time around. I know Sledge was pretty disappointed, but luckily I got him to understand the situation."

"What about Ben Forester? I heard he likes you?" Marta asked, eyes gleaming mischievously in the firelight.

"He does," supplied Marilee. "But Kelly is true-blue to Scott."

"C'mon." Kelly blushed and socked her friend playfully in the arm.

"One or two little dates can't hurt anything, Kelly," Lana encouraged. "Nobody can accuse you of not caring for Scott. You do. But you can't stop having fun. That's life, and you've never dated anyone but Scott, have you?"

"I never wanted to."

"I didn't think I wanted to before Joe and I broke up," Lana said. "I was a hermit for awhile afterward. But I'm having fun dating now. It's amazing how you get over a broken heart when you have to."

"This is a different kind of broken heart," Kelly explained.

"I think Ben is the best medicine for your malady," Lana said. "He's a real sweetie."

"Now that I have the blessing of my friends, I can do whatever I want?"

They all giggled. "Just about. Just ask us — we'll give our words of wisdom anytime."

A peace settled around Kelly with the knowledge that her friends were behind her, one hundred percent.

"I thought I told you not to come around." Scott scowled when he saw Kelly enter. She was wearing a light green skirt with a striped tie belt.

"I don't follow directions well," she returned, sitting down on an orange, spoon-shaped chair.

The therapist, Jackie, lifted Scott and

helped him over to the rails along which he would try to walk.

"I don't like to be watched," Scott said.

"You never rejected an audience before. Why is now so different? This is probably the hardest thing you've ever done in your life, except the difference is, your cheering section's changed slightly."

"Very funny." He was silent, concentrating on the movement of his legs, which was extremely limited.

Kelly watched, wincing at every painstaking step, trying to imagine what it was like to fight unwilling limbs. She was disappointed when Jackie had to help him along the last half.

"Congratulations. That was a vast improvement over yesterday," Jackie beamed.

"Kelly's not impressed, Jackie. I've got to do better than that."

"Kelly wasn't here yesterday. If she had been, she'd be amazed," Jackie insisted as Scott lowered himself into his chair.

Jackie hurried off to help someone else.

"How do you like it, Kelly? Not exactly your high school gymnasium, is it? No trampoline, for instance."

"You have tumbling mats," she noted, and he smiled. Her spirits rose. It had been so long since she'd seen him smile.

"Is that a new outfit?" he asked.

"Yes."

"Looks nice." He eyed her thoughtfully. "Anybody asked you out yet?"

"No, Scott," she lied. "Nobody."

"Would you go if they did ask you?"

"No, of course not." Kelly squirmed uncomfortably, thinking of Ben. The evening they'd spent dancing together was a vivid, sweet memory. She couldn't deny what she experienced in his arms. Quickly, she changed the subject. "Hey, did you ever think of covering sports for the school paper, Scott?"

"Where'd you get an idea like that?"

"Well, Ben Forester wanted to talk to you about it. He thought you might be interested. That way you can stay involved."

"D'you think I want to cover sports from a wheelchair? Gimp reporter, is that it? Kelly, don't you understand?"

"I'm trying to. But you keep yelling at me."

"Well, you're such a dummy. And I told you I don't want to see you."

"For some reason, I just can't stay away from you," she replied softly.

"Do me a favor and stay away." Scott closed his eyes. "When do the relays start?"

"This afternoon."

"Good. Who's swimming with you?"

"Ted Cummings."

"Breaststroke?"

"Yeah."

"Good."

"Wish you could be there."

"That'll be the day."

Time to change the subject again. "My mother was here."

"Good visit?"

"Yes." Kelly touched Scott's hand, knowing that he could feel and grasp quite well now. Perhaps he would never get back his fine finger dexterity, but she knew he could squeeze her hand and respond, if he wanted to. She longed for him to make some gesture, stroke her cheek or lean forward to kiss her, but he didn't.

Yet he didn't pull away when she touched him. She leaned over the arm of the chair and kissed him on the lips.

"Wish me luck, okay? I'm going to need it."

"Good luck," he returned gruffly, but there was the hint of a smile at the corners of his mouth, infusing her with hope.

Maybe everything would work out okay after all.

Kelly was nervous as she stared into the opal depths of the pool, surveying the reflections of her competition. Matt Prather, Joe Hammer, Janet Williamson, and Talia Wentz from Irwin High made a formidable team, especially since Scott was no longer swimming.

Clancy High had counted on Scott's performance this year to pull the team through, so everyone was feeling the pressure of his absence, knowing that the entire team had to work harder than ever to win.

Kelly could barely concentrate on Mr. Malmin's last-minute instructions. All the area high schools had preliminary relays such as these today, which paved the way for a big league competition later on. It was always exciting to see who was swimming and how well they did. Talia, with her swan-like, graceful manner, had won two consecutive diving titles and was expected to win a third this year.

In Kelly's category, breaststroke, she and Ted Cummings were pitted against Janet Williamson and Joe Hammer of Irwin, two swimmers they'd tied with in last year's league.

Kelly plowed through the pool, imagining Scott's smile at the end of each lap. How special and rare it was to see him smile — she hoped he'd start doing it more. To get Scott to feel again, in more ways than one — wasn't that part of the treatment?

Kelly swam fiercely, closing up the gap between swimmers, pushing herself out of the water a full length ahead of her opponent and Ted, to a jubilant Mr. Malmin.

"Great time, Kelly! You beat Irwin 2 to 1!"

Teammates crowded around, ecstatic at the new victory. Someone pushed through the mob; tall, self-assured, he planted a warm kiss on Kelly's chilled cheek.

"Congratulations, Kelly. Good show!" Ben announced proudly, eyes shining with unmasked admiration.

"Thanks," she whispered, the air vanishing from her lungs all of a sudden.

E^{leven}

Scott listened to Logan Murphy play his guitar, wanting to be transported a million miles away from the cluster of rapt faces, almost making you forget you were disabled.

He wanted to be free of this place, back with "normal" people. Of course, they all felt that way, except they still thought of themselves as they were before the accident. Acceptance was about the hardest thing in the world.

Already, Scott could see by comparison that he was better off than many of the patients. He had a good measure of return in his hands and arms, and he was getting return in his legs, which meant he stood a good chance of walking someday.

Logan Murphy had been a football jock before his accident. "Once a high school sweetheart," was how he described his past life, "now a paraplegic with no chance of walking." Besides himself, Logan seemed to be about the most bitter about what happened to him.

". . . Love is beyond me now. . . ." He ended the warbly chorus on a high note.

"Did you write that one, Logan?" asked Scott.

"Yeah. D'you like it? It's my new career. Writing love songs, about the old days . . . when I had a love life." He managed a wistful smile.

"D'you have a girlfriend?" Scott asked.

"Not anymore. My girlfriend couldn't take me being a cripple, so she took off. My friend, Tony, says she's got a new guy."

"That's too bad," Scott commiserated, thinking of Kelly.

"That's inevitable, man. How do you expect her to react? I was acting terrible towards her. She can do so much better than me, you know what I mean? Get another football captain or something. She's a cheerleader."

"I don't know about Kelly," Scott said. "I think she might be seeing someone else."

"Did you ask her? She seems really faithful. She's always visiting you," Logan reminded him.

"She denies it, so I guess I'll never know for sure. I just can't imagine why she'd want me now. I'm not exactly a prize." Scott stopped talking, afraid he was revealing too much of himself.

"You're both sports freaks, aren't you?"

"Yeah."

"So you think this is gonna change all that?"

"Isn't it?"

"Sure it is. Is she looking at that?"

"I don't know. I'm sure she realizes I'm not going to be the swim team champ or the tennis champ this year, or next. We're both pretty competitive, so those things are important. I can't help thinking how it could've been, you know? When I dream, I'm not a gimp. I'm walking . . . running, mostly."

"Yeah, me, too," Logan said. "Makes me prefer to dream. I get more accomplished."

Fear squirmed around in Scott's heart. If Logan had trouble with his girlfriend, then Scott wasn't wrong in expecting the same with Kelly. He knew it was just a matter of time before they broke up.

Maybe it would've been a lot easier if she'd just left him alone after the accident, instead of sticking around. He could've made a clean break — loss of girl, loss of function, all at the same time. Simple as that.

Kelly fairly skipped along the hallway of the rehab wing, breezing into Scott's room unannounced. "Guess what?"

"What're you doing here? It's dinnertime." He looked annoyed, she guessed because he didn't want her to see him fumble with his dinner tray.

"I had to let you know. We won the breast-stroke competition!"

"Hey, wait. You're upsetting the sliced peaches!"

Sure enough, peaches slid off the bowl into the tray.

Kelly scooped them up while she talked. "Oh, sorry. Isn't that exciting?"

"Oh, yeah, sure."

"You're not excited," she concluded, studying Scott's glum expression. *What's the matter with him? Doesn't he remember how important this is? If he were there, he would've won the freestyle.* "We lost the free-style. If you'd been there . . ."

"If I'd been there, you still would've lost. Cripples don't swim especially fast."

"Well, I mean . . ."

"If I was like I used to be, right?"

Kelly didn't answer. Her voice stuck in her throat.

"You can't keep thinking that way, Kelly. You've got to accept it. Doesn't that sound easy? Just accept it, stop fighting it — hah! I wish I could." The sea-green eyes met hers with searing honesty, which made her want to cry.

"We have to work it out, Scott. I know I'm not doing everything right, but between the two of us, we've got to work on us."

"Yeah, sure. It sounds good, but I don't think I've got the energy right now, Kelly. That's why I keep telling you to get lost. I think it's better that way, but you're so stubborn you won't listen. Nothing'll ever be the same again for us. The sooner you see it, the better off you'll be.

"Other people like me tell me their girls ditched out pretty early on. That seems like the smart thing to do."

Kelly swallowed hard. "I'm not giving up on you so easily, Scott. Don't you see that?"

She kissed him, but he moved his mouth away, leaving Kelly brushing her lips against his hair. "By the way, you're eating much better," she told him, but he refused to look at her.

Marilee met her in the hallway. "For God's sake, what happened this time?"

"C'mon, I'll tell you all about it. Let's just drive for awhile."

Marilee drove Kelly's car and did one of

the things she did best — listened. Kelly felt like all she'd been doing lately was dumping her problems on her dearest friend. But she also knew that as soon as Marilee had a problem, the tables would turn.

"The way I see it, Kelly, Scott is probably jealous because he knows that you're a success on the swim team, which he still wants to be, and he can't swim. Sure, he's happy for you in his own way, but it's hard because he sees you moving on ahead, leaving him in the dust. You can outdistance him in many ways, and he's really scared of that."

"There isn't anything I can do about it," Kelly said. "Unless I quit the team and quit everything."

Marilee looked at her sharply. "Don't you dare do that. If Scott's got to envy you for awhile, then let him. Don't you stop your life.

"By the way, speaking of life, I saw you after the meet with Ben. Care to elaborate?"

"Aren't you the nosey one? I guess I can't hide anything from your prying eyes."

"Your best friend knows everything."

"He wanted to take me out for a Coke, but I wanted to see Scott, so I said no. But he wants to take me out sometime." Kelly laid her head back against the headrest and closed her eyes. She really wanted to go with Ben and just forget the sense of obligation she had towards Scott, but it wouldn't go away.

Was it love or obligation, she wondered, that was holding her to Scott? Her whole life seemed warped by his injury. She no longer had time to fit in everything she had to do — school, practices, homework, and going to the hospital. In the end, which activity was going to suffer? Already she was about to lose her place on the tennis team. What next?

"I think you should go out with him," Marilee said softly.

"I told Scott I wasn't seeing anyone else. I don't want to lie."

"How long has it been since the accident?"

"I don't know . . . three and a half months, I think. It feels like forever."

"Yet you're still thinking as if it never happened."

"Right. In some ways, I am." Kelly opened her eyes and looked around. The terrain was unfamiliar, and it was dark. They were driving up into the hills. Through the bottlebrush branches of pines, they could see the Bay Area twinkling below, the lights of the Golden Gate Bridge strung like a jeweled necklace across a black expanse of water.

"Where are we, anyway?"

"The Oakland hills. I took the wrong turnoff back there, we were so busy talking. I just kept driving."

Kelly burst out laughing. "What do we do now?"

"Well, first, I think we'd better call home. And second, why don't we go into Berkeley and see a foreign film, with subtitles?"

"Can't we do that at home?"

"Sure . . . but there's a wider selection here. This'll be good for you, Kelly. You'll have to concentrate, so you'll forget all your troubles."

"Sounds like the perfect prescription for heartbreak," Kelly joked, gazing at the sparkling bay, remembering a happier time, when she and Scott had come up here on a field trip. It stood out in her memory because she recalled Ms. Engstrom, the science teacher, scolding them for kissing in the back of the school bus.

The sweet memory wrapped painfully around her heart. Kelly opened the window, breathing in lungfuls of cold night air to clear her head.

Twelve

"Kelly, this report card is awful! With the exception of PE, what you have here is C's, and I know you can do better than that," Mickey Horn complained to his daughter. He put two English muffins in the toaster.

"You know, Dad, we are a body-oriented society," Kelly quoted the psychologist.

"Well, I'd like to see you get less body-oriented and more brain-oriented. Otherwise, you're not going to be kept on the teams, you won't be able to get into a good college, and I'll have to drain that pool in the backyard."

An excessive person to begin with, her father smeared about a quarter of a stick of butter on the muffins.

"You should watch the butter, Dad. You don't need the cholesterol."

"If I need nutritional advice, I'll consult Jane Fonda, thank you."

"She's the workout expert. Does she have a diet, too?" Kelly giggled, hoping to throw her dad off the subject of grades.

"Smarty. But this doesn't solve the problem of the disgusting report card."

"Dad, if it makes you any happier, Sledgewick is benching me for the tennis tourney because I haven't shown up for a bunch of practices. Luckily, I have a pool, so I don't miss as much swim practice."

"Would it help if I installed a tennis court back there, too?" Mickey grinned around a mouthful of muffin.

"Ha-ha. Very funny."

"I know Scott's injury is beginning to wear you down, Kelly. You don't have to say so." He turned his back to her, pouring coffee. "It's evident in your whole life. I think it's changing you."

"Yeah, well, I'm sure there's a pot of gold at the end of the rainbow." She tried to make a joke of it, but it flopped.

"Certainly, yet it may not be the pot you're expecting. You should start considering what it's going to be like after Scott gets home, if his attitude doesn't improve. And if he doesn't make good progress, where will that put you? You aren't tied to him, you know," he said softly.

"Dad, are you trying to tell me I don't have to love him if I don't want to?"

"I don't know. I just know I don't like seeing you pulled down by this. Sure, you feel a certain responsibility for Scott, and love, but I'm not certain where one starts and the other leaves off. So maybe you need to examine those feelings, and above all, I think you need to have some fun, so that you have a way of putting this all in perspective."

"Dad, everybody keeps telling me to have fun. I'm doing okay."

"I'm proud of you, Kelly. You're terrific. What you've done for Scott so far has been wonderful. But he's doing all the taking and you all the giving. It can't go on that way forever. You'll grow tired of it. You'll see."

Kelly picked up her backpack and silently slung it over her shoulder.

"Don't worry." With reluctance, her dad signed the report card and handed it to her. "Even if you get absolutely lousy grades, I won't drain the pool."

Kelly grinned at him before she walked out the door. "Oops — ace reporter has jam on his tie," she giggled, cleaning up the dripping jam.

"Can you get a ride home after school, Kelly? I'm going home with Chuck," said

Marilee as Kelly jumped into her bright yellow Ford.

"Sure, no problem," muttered Kelly, feeling lonesome all of a sudden. Lately, she counted a lot on Marilee when she was feeling blue.

"We're studying together tonight." Marilee shot Kelly a sly grin. "And practicing my new play."

"Looks like you'll get a lot of studying done," Kelly remarked. "I notice you're wearing your new punky skirt today."

Marilee was into weird put-togethers and exotic color combinations that she somehow managed to pull off. "Do you think he'll like it?"

"He'll either like it or run screaming in the opposite direction." Which was about the most honest statement Kelly could make about the bright green, tight skirt and bright pink belt.

"I'll let you know how he reacts."

"Meaning, I may get a ride home after all," Kelly interpreted, laughing.

Ben was waiting for her when she got to her locker. He looked especially nice in a blue pin-striped shirt and new jeans.

"Hi. I knew if I hung out here long enough, I'd get to see you this morning."

"You look nice."

"Thanks. This is my I'm-going-to-ask-

Kelly-Horn-out outfit." He grinned, and Kelly couldn't help but laugh.

"Oh, okay."

"Does that mean okay, you'll go out with me?"

"No, it means okay, you're wearing your ask-me-out clothes."

"But how can you resist?"

He was behind her as she worked her combination, and she caught a whiff of his cologne wafting over her.

"You or your appearance?" she asked teasingly.

"The entire package!"

They both laughed.

"Listen, I'm not sure about the date, but maybe you can give me a ride home after school?" Kelly asked, her face flushing.

"Love to. It'll give me a chance to talk you into the date."

Kelly looked forward to after school. She met Ben at her locker, and they walked along the footbridge that led to the back parking lot where he kept his car. It had rained during lunch period, so the branches were laced with raindrops, which brushed off into Ben's hair as they strolled.

"Can we get a Coke? Do you have time?" he wanted to know, opening the door of a cute MG.

"I really shouldn't, Ben. I've got to go to the hospital."

"How do you get your homework done with all this running around? I'd be a wreck by now."

"It's not easy. My grades are suffering," she admitted, recalling her report card.

"How about the sports? Can you keep up?"

She explained about the tennis coach benching her, which was a big disappointment but one she just had to live with at the moment. "Some things are more important than tennis," she sighed.

"Like Scott Martin?" Ben smiled and put his hand over hers. "I really wish you didn't like him so much."

"Oh?"

"Hmmm. But then I think that's one of the admirable things about you, Kelly. Besides the fact that you're pretty, an excellent swimmer, tennis player . . ."

"Keep going. I thrive on flattery." She laughed.

"Good sense of humor, likes animals . . ."

"How do you know that?"

"Oh, I just guessed. I can't imagine you being mean to animals, and I know you've got a good sense of humor."

"Because I laugh at your corny jokes?"

"Sure, why not?" Then he proceeded to tell

her one: "What goes like this?" He snapped his fingers in a wide circle.

"I don't know," Kelly sighed.

"A butterfly with hiccups."

She laughed.

"See what a sense of humor you have?"

"Either that or I'm just as crazy as you are."

"Scott's really lucky that you stick with him."

It's too bad Scott doesn't realize that, Kelly thought to herself.

They were silent, roaring comfortably along a country road, a long way to Kelly's house. Leaves spiraled to the ground and seemed to crowd in drifts in the gutters, while farmland stretched on both sides of the road, separated by the stitches of barbed-wire fencing.

When they arrived at Kelly's house, Ben leaned over as if he was going to kiss her, drawing very close. Kelly held her breath, not knowing whether she wanted him to or not.

"What about the date?" he persisted. "Yes or no?"

"Call me tonight, okay?" Ben looked disappointed, so Kelly amended. "I can't make up my mind right now, Ben."

He nodded. "I understand. You'll hear from me tonight."

* * *

"This morning when I was in the elevator, a lady looked down at me and —"

"Don't you love being looked down at?" Scott interrupted.

"Yeah . . . and she said she had a close friend who was in a wheelchair."

Everybody broke up laughing.

"Yeah, we all have close friends who're in wheelchairs."

Sarah Metcalf, the girlfriend of Kyle Wembley, shook her head in disbelief. She was around seventeen, slender and tall, with red hair and a bubbly personality. Kyle was a really sweet boy who had been in a motorcycle wreck, leaving him a quadriplegic with very little return in any of his limbs.

"Well, it's better than being ignored," Sarah said brightly. "Isn't that what you're always complaining about, being ignored?"

Scott wiped his eyes on his sleeve. It was the first time he'd had a good laugh in ages. And imagine — laughing over these horrible chrome cages they were stuck in!

"What's everyone laughing about?"

Kelly stood in the doorway, looking perplexed. She'd never met a lot of the people in rehab, so Scott introduced everybody — Kyle and Sarah, Manuel, Merrie, and Logan.

"Nice to meet you all."

"Kelly's a great athlete, aren't you, Kelly?" Scott prodded her.

"So are you, Scott."

He sensed the irritation in her voice. She acted like she was on the verge of tears a lot lately. He hated to see that, and maybe he'd been ignoring those signposts. But he was looking at her now, and seeing her awfully clearly.

"Scott's been showing us some arm-wrestling techniques," said Manuel, which made everybody giggle. Manuel couldn't move his arms at all.

Kelly didn't laugh. She missed the joke or, more likely, to her way of thinking it wasn't a joke at all. "Will you ever get return in your arms?" she asked him.

"Maybe," he replied.

She looked uncomfortable.

"These guys are pulling your leg," Merrie said, which elicited fresh chuckles. "At least, I should say, they'd like to be able to get up and do just that."

Sarah clapped her hands together in obvious glee. "Merrie, you're a ray of sunshine in here."

"Somebody has to be. These guys are enough to make me feel like a cripple."

Kelly winced, which didn't go unnoticed by Scott. "Kelly doesn't like our terminology, I guess. 'Crip' or 'cripple' is a term used with fondness, the same as 'gimp.' We love being the way we are," he explained sarcastically.

"Oh, come on, Scott. Don't be mean," Merrie scolded him. "Part of what he says is right, though, Kelly. 'Wheeler' is another term."

"You've got no idea what it's like to wheel around admiring belt buckles," Scott teased, shooting a glance Kelly's way.

"It must be frustrating." Kelly tried to commiserate.

"You haven't known what it's like since you were a little kid. That's the level we're at," Manuel offered, smiling.

"Nobody treats you like a kid, do they, Scott?" Kelly asked.

Scott was suddenly embarrassed by her attentions. Everyone looked at him for an answer. Scott realized he was afraid of Kelly — afraid of her being here, afraid of her never coming back. What did he want, anyway?

"No, they don't. But I keep hearing how weird it is once you get out of the hospital."

Scott pretended not to notice Kelly rest her hand on his arm. He wheeled away.

"I'm going home now, Scott," she said, her face crumpling, indicating she was going to cry. His heart twisted into a knot, because he knew she rarely cried. She had once, when her cat had caught a virus and had to be put to sleep, but that wasn't his fault, and he'd comforted her then.

He wanted to comfort her now, but he held back, deciding it would be easier on both of them if he didn't.

"Bye," he said, and everyone else chimed in, diminishing his into something less personal.

Kelly left the bright room, not realizing Sarah followed her.

"I felt the same way when Kyle first went through this," Sarah told Kelly. They sat outside on the half-moon of lawn near the entrance. "They're bitter; they don't want sympathy and yet they ask for it in every word and gesture."

"How long's he going to be like this?" Kelly asked.

"You mean, crippled or a big pain?"

Kelly tried to smile. "A big pain."

"It depends. Some people never get past that stage, but most do. If you want to have any kind of life after an injury, you get yourself together. But you know Scott has to go through all this depression first, right? Has he told you to shove off yet?"

"Lots of times."

"Hey, Tom. How're you doing?" Sarah waved to a young orderly, who brightened when he saw her. "Well, that's good. That shows you have stick-to-it-iveness. He'll start to notice that you're sticking by him even though he's unbearable. That counts for a lot in the long run."

"It's nice to know I'm not the only person going through this, although I wouldn't wish it on anybody," Kelly said. "Of course, his mother's going through it, too, but it's different."

"It's a lot different. For one thing, guys aren't used to being in a helpless or dependent role. They're not well trained to be sick, though I wonder where people get the idea women are. Doctors always think women make better patients. But a guy can feel more comfortable letting his mother help him out than his girlfriend."

"I can see that," Kelly said.

"Scott is really a lucky guy. It's too bad he doesn't realize it," Sarah said.

"His attitude's working against him."

"He'll pick up on it pretty soon. He's really scared right now." Sarah scooped her red hair out of her eyes and nodded to a row of wheelchairs lined up inside the door. "Why don't I take you for a ride? It'll give you an idea of what these people have to live with."

Sarah went through the whole routine of showing Kelly how she'd have to lift her slack legs and fit them into the footholds, where the brake was, and how to push the chair.

"You can get motorized ones, but we don't

want you to get lazy," was Sarah's explanation.

They wheeled across the grounds and into the pharmacy.

"Why are we going in here?" Kelly wanted to know.

"I want a candy bar." Sarah picked one out and handed it to Kelly to pay for. While Kelly dug in her purse for change, the druggist addressed Sarah.

"Can I help you?" he asked as if he didn't even see Kelly!

"My friend would like to pay for this candy bar," Sarah announced, pointing at Kelly.

"Oh, I'm sorry." He blushed, suddenly apologetic, and leaned over the counter to take her money.

"He didn't even notice me," Kelly exclaimed once they were outside.

"See how it is? I think it would bug you after awhile."

They wheeled the chair back to its parking space, and Sarah scribbled her phone number on a scrap of binder paper.

"Give me a call if you need to talk. And don't let these gimps get to you."

Kelly smiled gratefully. "Thanks."

Thirteen

"Well, what's your answer? I feel as if I'm chasing a rainbow," Ben joked, but Kelly could tell he was uneasy.

"Maybe you are," she responded, the weight of the last hour pulling her down. "When do you want to go out? This weekend? How does that sound?" Kelly asked.

The weekend was far enough away, Kelly figured, that she could break the date if necessary. Right now she didn't feel like it, but anything could happen by the weekend.

"Okay?"

"Saturday night," Ben said. "I'll call again and we can decide on what we want to do." They talked for a few minutes longer, then her father had to use the phone.

"Hot date, huh?" he quipped, nudging her with his elbow. "You and Scott have a fight?" he pressed when she didn't reply.

"Scott and I never get along anymore, Dad," she grumbled. "He's such a grouch . . ." She bit off the rest of the sentence, not wanting to spill all her complaints.

"He's such a grouch you don't know whether you want to bother with him anymore?" Her dad finished the sentence with his own brand of straightforwardness.

"That's what makes you a good newspaperman, Dad. You're so direct, painfully direct," Kelly returned. "Naturally, you realize it isn't as simple as that."

"Of course not. Nothing's simple." He made a quick phone call, sounding almost brusque, which Kelly had never gotten used to. He explained that news people have to learn to get on and off the phone fast, but a lot of people didn't understand and thought he was being rude.

"By the way, I've got a date, too," Kelly's father said.

"With whom?"

"I'm flying to New York to be with your mother. I really miss her. You have her number, right?"

"Yes."

"You'll be okay by yourself?"

"Yes. I'm sixteen, not six."

"Keep forgetting. Let's see. Bolt the doors, don't forget to pick up messages . . ."

"Brush my teeth, don't talk to strangers, and don't eat too much junk food."

"You got it. How'd I produce such a smart kid?"

"Incredible genes." Carrying his suitcase to the side door, he turned to her. "See you Friday."

After he was gone, Kelly felt really alone. Often, she wished for the house to herself when her dad was driving her crazy with his cassette tapes of interviews blaring through the bathroom speakers, but she wasn't sure she liked it so quiet now.

She phoned Marilee.

"Sounds like you've got a case of the blahs," deduced her friend. "Why don't you come over? My mother won't notice one more airhead around."

"You're so complimentary, Marilee."

Marilee's household was a riot of activity. Her twin red-headed sisters, Linda and Laura, ten years old, were chasing each other through the house.

"Where's your mother?" Kelly asked.

"Oh, she locked herself in her bédroom. I think she's getting packed to leave," Marilee said, smiling.

The two girls spent the evening laughing, negotiating the Monopoly board, and eating until they felt sick. Laura and Linda were sent to their room to do homework, which sent the noise level down a few decibels.

"It's not just your dad leaving that's got you down, is it?" Marilee asked.

Kelly had forgotten how bad she felt earlier, but she told Marilee about Sarah and the rehab center. "I got uptight when they started joking about their disabilities. I mean, I can't see where it's funny."

"I guess they figure they either laugh or cry."

"It's some kind of defense, I guess. Sarah says, 'Don't let these gimps get to you.' "

Marilee laughed. "That's funny. Who would ever think?"

"I know. It's amazing."

"Hey, why don't you spend the night? I bet you don't want to drive home to that big, empty house."

Kelly shook her head. Marilee must have been reading her mind.

"C'mon. I'll find you a pair of pajamas."

Although Kelly didn't see that much of her father when he was in town, just knowing the house was empty made her seek ways to stay out. Instead of studying at home, she stayed at the library until it closed. Then she grabbed a hamburger on the way home.

She nearly moved into Marilee's, and if Marilee hadn't had a date with Chuck Thursday night, she would have stayed until Friday.

That evening she went to visit Scott, who told her he'd be leaving the hospital in a couple of weeks and be coming in as a regular outpatient. It would be five months since his accident.

"Aren't you happy?" Kelly asked, thinking this was a major achievement.

He shrugged. "What can I do out there that I can't do here? It just means I'll have more to worry about."

"That's a lousy attitude," she scolded.

"Who cares?"

"Why don't you talk to Dr. Rodriguez?"

"Do you think I'm crazy?" he asked.

"*No*, I think you just need to talk to someone who can help you sort out your feelings," Kelly said firmly.

The next couple of weeks were very difficult with Scott. To her knowledge, he didn't speak to Dr. Rodriguez, or if he had, it didn't do any good. Kelly canceled her date with Ben, explaining that Scott was getting out of the hospital.

"I sort of thought you would say that, Kelly, but I understand." Ben chuckled softly. "I almost wish I was in Martin's shoes sometimes."

"Don't ever wish that," Kelly said angrily.

"I'm sorry. I didn't mean it how it sounded. Another time?"

"Sure, another time would be fine."

How long is he going to understand? Kelly wondered, realizing her own patience was getting frayed over Scott. She even wondered if Dr. Rodriguez was wrong in suggesting she stick by him. What if he didn't change his attitude? Did the old Scott she used to know still exist at all?

Lately, Kelly wasn't sure he did.

Fourteen

"Happy Homecoming!"

"How do you like it?" Scott's mother moved uneasily from one foot to the other, motioning to the blue-and-white crepe paper streamers looping their way across the dining room. A big poster hung over the mantelpiece, obliterating the African woodcuts. It read: WELCOME HOME, SCOTT.

Scott received this display with a dark scowl. "I'm glad you didn't invite the neighbors. I mean, it's a relief not being a main attraction."

"Scott . . ." Kelly seethed, taken aback by his sarcasm.

Mrs. Martin's mouth tightened imperceptibly, but she said nothing, turning her back on her son to put last-minute decorations on the cake. Besides Kelly and Mrs. Martin, Scott's older brothers, Ken and Steven, were present, and Kelly had invited Manuel, since he was the only disabled friend of Scott's who was out of the hospital. Also, she was hoping Manuel's presence would be good for Scott.

"I bet it's been a long time since you've had homemade chocolate cake," Kelly said, trying to make idle conversation.

"No, it hasn't. Sarah brought one in for Kyle's birthday. You missed it, Kelly. One of the highlights of my stay in the hospital."

"I'm sure it wasn't as good as your mother's," Manuel put in, winking at Mrs. Martin.

Kelly bit back her fury. She'd spent two whole art periods creating the huge poster for this occasion, and Mrs. Martin had made Scott's favorite cake, and he was deliberately trying to hurt them.

"Just think how nice it will be to have chocolate cake more often, Scott," Kelly suggested just to make conversation. "Are you on a special diet?"

"Not really, but I'll have to be if everyone keeps feeding me."

"Still the old Bottomless Pit?" She tried the old joke on him.

"There is the problem of weight gain, you know," Mrs. Martin informed Kelly.

I already know that, Kelly fumed inwardly. But poor Mrs. Martin was nervous and trying to make everything turn out right.

"Have you had any problem with your weight, Scott?" Kelly asked casually. "You don't look as though you've gained."

"Glad you asked. It gets annoying being discussed as if I wasn't here." He shook his head, and Kelly noticed that the shaved spots of hair were growing in nicely and blending with the rest. "No, I haven't had trouble. Hospital food isn't exactly French cuisine, you know."

Kelly giggled. "As long as you get your exercise, you should be okay."

"Yeah. I can do laps around the block — on my head."

"Sarcastic, but funny." Kelly had another slim piece of cake. She was thinking how she'd like to mash it in Scott's face.

"Kelly, I really have to thank you for being such a help to Scott during this time." Mrs. Martin spoke in a low tone so the others didn't hear. "I don't know how he would've made it through without you. You've been a true inspiration."

"I'm not sure of that, Mrs. Martin." Kelly shook her head in dismay. "At times I think

I've been more trouble to Scott than anything. He doesn't seem to care whether I'm
around or not."

"He cares a lot, but he just can't show anybody he cares right now. I just pray he gets
over this soon, so he can enjoy the rest of his
life." Tears filled her eyes, and Kelly noticed
how much older she looked since Scott's
accident. Lines fanned out from her eyes into
her hairline, and her face had a pinched
quality it never had before.

"He will." Kelly gave her a confident smile.

After an uncomfortable silence in which
they all picked politely at their cake, Kelly
excused herself. "I have to get going. I've got
a biology test to study for and I've got to
swim. Thanks for the party and the cake,
Mrs. Martin. It was really delicious."

"D'you mean you're going to leave us here
with this grouchy gimp, Kelly?" Manuel
teased.

Ken and Steven blushed up to their hair
roots. Kelly guessed they felt as uncomfortable as she once did about their brother being
referred to as a "gimp." She'd watched the
two older boys skirt Scott's chair, asking him
if he needed anything, very solicitous, but
careful, as if they thought their brother
might break.

*That's how I treat him. I mince around
him, trying not to upset him, but I do anyway.*

Kelly said good-bye. Outside in the rain, she leaned her hot face upward into the wind, yet it couldn't cool her anger. It was becoming increasingly difficult to remember just what she loved about Scott in the first place.

"Hi."

"Hi." Ben's voice vibrated deep and resonant across the phone wire, restoring Kelly's faith in mankind. "How are you?"

"Oh, fine."

"D'you feel like going out?" He paused. "I'm beginning to sound like a broken record. Pretty soon, I'll just call you up and turn on my recorded message."

Kelly laughed. "It varies. I don't think you have to go that far."

They went skating along the wooded footpaths in the park. Kelly had spent many hours at a local roller rink with Scott and was very agile on skates, which Ben was not.

"You're skating circles around me," he complained, landing with a painful thud on his butt. "Can we do something else? Something gentle? I'm liable to get hurt."

"I don't want to be responsible for that." Kelly giggled, offering her hand. "Why don't we get an ice cream?"

Ben couldn't get his skates off fast enough.

The Big Scoop ice-cream parlor was crowded with Clancy kids, and Kelly immediately felt self-conscious walking in with Ben. A few people she knew said hi, studying the couple.

Ben touched her elbow lightly, as if to reassure her it was okay. He chose a corner table. "Don't be nervous. I'll order for us, okay?"

While he was gone, Kelly fumbled with a sugar packet, unable to help overhearing a conversation a couple of booths away.

"I thought she was going with Scott Martin."

"Yes, but you heard about Scott's accident, didn't you? He's *paralyzed*."

"How bad is he? A basket case?"

Somebody giggled.

"Do you think they're not going together anymore?"

"Who knows? It sorta looks that way."

"I wonder how Ben feels about it."

"*Shhh*. She might hear."

Just then Ben returned with a huge banana split. "Let's see who can finish first." He grinned, handing her a spoon.

Kelly forced a smile, even though she wanted to cry. How could they talk that way about her and Scott? They had no idea what it was like between them, what Scott had become, what he had gone through.

"Hey, Kelly, what's up? You're not smiling." Ben eyed her with concern, blotting ice cream from his lips.

"Everything's fine. But I wonder, after we finish this, can we leave?"

"Well, sure." Disappointment shone in his eyes. "I thought you might want to dance or something."

"No, it's really noisy in here . . ."

They ate in silence, and it seemed to Kelly to take forever to get to the bottom of the banana boat. Ben lingered, waiting for Kelly to catch up.

"I'm saving some for you. I don't want you nicknaming me 'Oink.' "

Kelly laughed. "Eat it all. I'll never be able to finish."

They left, the object of many surreptitious glances as they passed through the sliding glass doors.

"Nothing like feeling like you're in a fish-bowl," declared Kelly, taking a deep breath.

"What gave you that impression? Was it the glass?" Architecturally, the Big Scoop was composed mainly of plate glass.

"No. The kids inside." She told him about the conversation she overheard.

"Tacky," Ben fumed. "When will people learn to keep their mouths shut?"

"Even if they did, Ben, I'd know what they were thinking just by the way they stared at us when we walked in there."

"Oh, yeah? I didn't pay attention."

"Well, you don't feel on parade. While Scott was in the hospital, people asked about him every day. Then after awhile, they stopped, and even stopped talking to me. Now, they'll start talking about us again, and about you and me."

"That's not necessarily so," Ben disagreed.

"I just know what they're thinking: she dumped Scott because he's paralyzed. I mean — isn't that the first thing that would come to your mind if you saw what they just saw?"

Ben turned slightly red, and Kelly thought maybe she had gone too far. "They might just be curious, Kelly."

"But they're making deductions." Tears rose to her eyes.

"You know how you feel about me and Scott, so what difference does it make what they think?"

He waited for her to answer, but she couldn't, so he went on talking. "You just don't feel right about it, I know. Listen, I didn't expect you to forget all about him. Of course, I kind of hoped you might get to like me more in time, but I just wanted to spend some time with you."

Kelly dabbed at her eyes with a Kleenex. "I'm sorry, Ben. I didn't mean to make a mess of this for you. I'm usually a lot happier, but this has really gotten to me."

"Hey." He rested his hand on hers, fingers sliding down to squeeze her palm. "I understand. You don't have to give me a big explanation. Here you are, delivered safely to your door."

"Thanks. And thanks for the nice time," Kelly sniffled, feeling totally dumb.

Ben wiped a stray tear from her cheek. "Liar." But his grin let her know that it was okay.

F*ifteen*

"I haven't seen Scott in rehab lately. Where's he been?" Sarah asked casually.

The two girls were sunning themselves in Kelly's backyard.

"Really? I thought he'd keep up with it, Sarah. He knows how important it is."

"Maybe his mommy's doing everything for him. That happened with Kyle. 'Helpless' became his middle name."

"Oh, no." *Mrs. Martin could be the perfect victim for that kind of setup,* Kelly thought. She hadn't spoken to Scott for a couple of days, but each time she phoned, Mrs. Martin said he was resting or couldn't come to the phone, so Kelly guessed he wanted to be alone

— which was just fine with her, because she wasn't sure she wanted to see him.

But this was something she had to talk to him about. She had to help him. He couldn't just sit around and waste away.

At the bottom of the handout Kelly received at the hospital was a list of referral agencies for the disabled. She called some and went to work.

By five o'clock the next afternoon, she had collected a heap of material to educate Scott on adapting to the outside world, and she marched over to his house.

"What're you doing here?" he demanded, finding her unannounced on the front step.

"I've got some information for you."

Scanning the headings, he frowned. "I did a lot of reading in the hospital." He wheeled in front of her, and she resisted the urge to push his chair.

"But you're acting like it doesn't apply to you. Are you taking care of yourself?"

"That's none of your business!"

"I know you're not going to rehab," Kelly said.

"Who told you? A little birdy?"

"I have ways of finding out. You need to get out of that chair and exercise. Did you know your sense of self-worth is tied up in taking care of your own body?" Kelly lifted that phrase right out of a manual. "It's a simple thing to do, but it means a lot."

"A lot to you maybe, but not to me."

"Did you know, for instance, that you can drive a car? Did you know there are swim ramps for the disabled, so that you can float a person on or off a wheelchair? Did you know that Berkeley's one of the easiest places for the handicapped to live?"

He gave her a funny look. "Are you suggesting I move?"

"No, just offering information." Kelly ruffled her sheets of paper. "I'm not denying anymore, Scott. I'm accepting what's happened to you — how about you?"

He shrugged.

"It would be good for you to get out and do more. Why don't you come to the swim meet? A lot of people would like to see you."

"I don't want to see them," he stated.

Kelly knew he'd been cold toward Mark Hunt and Rich Dixon, his close friends on the team. He needed to keep his old friends — didn't he realize that?

"Someday, you'll wish you hadn't said that," she ventured. "And if you stay in this house all day, you're going to get more bored and more miserable. You can only watch so many reruns on television before you go nuts. I know you — you'll need more stimulation than that. How many soap operas can Scott

watch? Want to count? I can come over after
school and you can tell me what happened on
Live Tomorrow."

Scott groaned and covered his eyes.

"Before you decide to curl up in a little
ball and die, here's the school newspaper, so
you can keep up with what's happening in
the outside world. You might ask Ben
Forester about writing for the sports section.
He may not want you anymore, I don't know.
There's also a wheelchair sports organiza-
tion, did you know about that? Anyway, if
you don't try to help yourself, Scott —"
Kelly couldn't finish her sentence. Tears got
in the way.

"You won't want me anymore, is that it?"
he questioned softly. "It's okay, Kelly. You
should've let go of me long ago."

"I mean it, Scott," she whispered. "I love
you, but it's getting harder, and I know it's
hard for you, but you've got to *try*."

When she was gone, Scott felt her absence
acutely, as if a cold gust of wind had blown
part of him away. He missed her, though he'd
talked himself into living without her. He
had no future, so there was no sense in
teasing himself with dreams of Kelly, and
there was no sense in rehab, which would
take forever and for what? For what?

Angrily, he charged around the house in

his chair, knocking against the furniture, upsetting potted plants.

"Scott, what're you doing? Be careful! You might hurt yourself!" his mother cried in alarm.

Her words galvanized him into action. He slammed his chair down the front stairs, across the lawn to the driveway, wheeled to the back patio then down four steps, and spilled onto the lawn. Mrs. Martin rushed out to see what happened.

"Scott, please! Stop! Are you trying to kill yourself?"

"Leave me alone! Let me help myself!" he ordered, hauling himself back into the chair. "Mom, you can't do everything for me. I'm not a kid. Just a gimp, that's all."

He wheeled away from her. Tears dried on his face as he sped down the street, wheeling up and down curbs, nearly tipping, exhilaration pounding through his veins. His lips stuck to his teeth as he drove the chair faster against the wind. At the side of one circular drive was a set of six stairs that he decided to brave.

Breaking down barriers — he had to break them down before he could move at all — wasn't that the name of the game? Mobility. He wanted it. He saw people walking around, taking their mobility for granted, and it

drove him crazy. He wanted to be them, he
envied them, he wished he could trade places
with them just for an hour.

Scott maneuvered the wheelchair down an
incline behind his house, carefully skirting
rocks and potholes, feeling in control. For
once, he was feeling in control. *You can't let
other people take care of every area of your
life; Kelly was right about that. Even if you
are a cripple.*

The chair squeaked and jolted, finally
spewing him out at the bottom of the hill,
sending him into a crumpled heap.

Scott dragged himself back to the chair.
Kelly had been trying to get through to him
for a long time. She said she accepted what
had happened. She might not understand
completely, but then who was he to expect it?
She'd stuck by him through this whole
ordeal, and he wasn't willing to go the rest
of the way with her? How would he feel if
he just let her go, without trying, without
making some effort to reach out for what they
once had together, to make sure it wasn't
lost forever?

He swiped at his eyes, annoyed with himself for crying, annoyed with every ounce of
his weakness. He'd been feeling so sorry for
himself, he couldn't accept anyone's sympathy. He was doing it all, that's what Dr.

Rodriguez said. He couldn't blame Kelly if she never wanted to see him again, after the way he'd acted.

No, I'm not going to be helpless, he railed at himself. *I'm going to be whole in as many ways as I can be. I* am *going to walk.*

Scott wheeled home furiously, past wide-eyed children and curious adults, up the front walkway, bounding over the threshold and into his room, where he struggled into his braces.

"Scott, you need help getting into those."

"No, Mom, just let me do it. You've got to let me." He was breathing hard, as if he'd run the fifty-yard dash.

"I was worried about you. I thought you had hurt yourself."

"Stop worrying." He stood shakily in the braces, leaned over, and left a big kiss on his mother's cheek. "I'm going to be just fine, Mom. Thanks . . . for caring."

"Oh, Scott. . . ." She couldn't finish, for seeing him wobbling on the braces filled her heart and pushed words right out of her mind.

"We're rooting for you, love." Kelly's father tousled her hair.

Kelly was nervous. The weather for the finals was bleak, gray clouds quilting the sky and threatening rain. There were thirty-five swimmers participating in the fifty-yard Junior/Senior freestyle, which was not Kelly's strongest stroke. At the last minute, Mark Hunt had to drop out due to an injury, so she was taking his place.

Glancing up at the bleachers, Kelly saw her father and then her mother, frantically waving a scarf. She waved back, heartened by her mother's appearance. Her mom had flown out to the West Coast for the swim meet, and Kelly loved her for it.

A hush fell over the crowd as the participants readied, taking their positions. Kelly plunged into the water, slicing rhythmically, her strokes sharp and definite — better than they'd been in a long time. She savored it — the control of her body, the dolphin-dive at the end of a lap, the way she shot through the water like a fish. *If I couldn't do this, like Scott . . .*

She'd been trying not to think of him since leaving his house yesterday, consciously turning her thoughts to this competition. If she could just remove him from her heart. . . .

The Clancy cheering section went wild as two of their swimmers, Kelly and Rich Dixon, finished first and second. Jubilant faces blurred before Kelly as she rose from the water. But what caught her eye was not the crowd's ecstasy, but one person in particular — Scott in his wheelchair, next to Darren Peterson.

Kelly blinked a few times to make sure she wasn't seeing a mirage. He'd shown up! She wanted to burst.

With renewed zest, she charged into the Varsity 100 breaststroke unflaggingly, finishing well ahead of her competitors.

While the scores were being chalked up, Mr. Malmin approached Kelly. "Did you see Scott? Boy, am I glad he came."

"Yeah, me, too. I thought he'd never show up."

"We're pleased to announce the winners of the Junior/Senior fifty-yard freestroke: Richard Dixon, first place; Kelly Horn, second . . . and for the Varsity 100 breaststroke, Kelly Horn, first place."

"I can't believe it!" Kelly yelled.

Regina glided toward her and wrapped a thick new towel about her shoulders. "Congratulations, darling! Isn't it wonderful?"

"You were terrific, Kelly." Her father's pet names came out at the most inopportune times.

"Dad . . ." Kelly frowned but was too happy to berate him for his slip.

Marilee and Chloe ran over to congratulate her.

"You were great, Kelly! We knew you could do it! What a performance!"

"To the champ," Ben said quietly, and Kelly wondered why he looked a little sad.

In all the confusion, she didn't notice Scott wheeling over to her side.

"Congratulations, K.H. You were fantastic." Scott grinned and squeezed her forearm.

A jolt sizzled up her arm from where he touched her, warming her all over. It had been so long since he'd demonstrated any affection.

"You splashed them dead," Scott added, not letting her go.

"Scott, it's so good to see you here. . . ." Kelly faltered, not knowing how to thank him for coming.

Shivering, she pulled the towel closer. "Why did you come?" she asked, remembering yesterday's scene.

He lifted a tape recorder from his lap. "This is my first assignment," he explained softly, his eyes making her want to melt — like they used to do.

Simultaneously, they burst out laughing, their laughter binding them together and separating them from everyone else.

Sixteen

"Want to go for a ride?"

Kelly held the receiver away from her ear, for a minute not believing it was Scott speaking. "W-with you?" she gasped. She had just returned from Marilee's play, which was a howling success. A group of kids were planning to go out later and celebrate.

"Who else? Mom and I traded in the Toyota for a new one, rigged up specially for gimps. Wanna try it out with me?"

"Sure."

A few minutes later, there was a familiar honk-honk-honk outside, the signal Scott always used when picking her up for dates. Kelly's spirits soared as she raced out to greet him, and seeing his profile in the car and that wonderful, happy grin again made her want to shout with joy.

She threw her arms around him. "Oh, Scott! I'm ecstatic!"

He revved the engine, a see-what-I-can-do look in his eye. "Jump in. I'm going to hot-rod for you."

The car was a pale blue Camaro, just sporty enough to command attention as it bellowed down Catalina Avenue. Heads turned as Scott turned onto the main street of town, and kids from school recognized him, their mouths flopping open at the sight.

"This is fun," he crowed, gunning the motor.

"They don't believe it's really you," Kelly said, laughing. She looked over at the contraption that hooked onto the brake and accelerator to make the car hand-controlled. "I can drive just as well as anybody now," Scott exclaimed. "It's not exactly a breeze getting in and out of this thing with a chair, but it's better than staying home. I'm starting swimming with Malmin next week. It'll be good to get back in the water again."

"I'm so glad," Kelly breathed. "You must have read about the swimming competitions for the disabled?"

"I did. I'm going to do sports reporting for the paper, too. I'm not much of a writer, but Ben thinks I can do it." Talking to Ben,

Scott sensed he had a soft spot for Kelly, but he decided not to ask her about it. He didn't want to do anything to spoil their fun.

"Want to see a movie?" Scott asked.

"Are you sure you're up to it?" Kelly answered softly.

"I'm up to anything right now, Kelly."

"Really, Scott, all I want to do is sit and talk. We haven't done that in a long time."

They parked on a cliff overlooking the entire city, which looked like a mini-kingdom as the shadows deepened and the lights popped on. Scott turned off the ignition and slid his arm around Kelly's shoulders.

"You know, I wanted to die so many times since the accident, and I know I'll feel that way every once in a while. Some days you just feel like a cripple, and others you feel great.

"I can't tell you it's fun being a gimp, but I think I'm finding my way up. I still have my life." The look he turned to Kelly was long and probing, and he thought, *How could I ever turn her away? She's so perfect, so alive.* "If it wasn't for you . . ."

"You've got your own strength, Scott. It doesn't have anything to do with me," she explained. "You just had to find it and tap it, that's all."

"No, you had a lot to do with it. I told you to leave me because I loved you and I wanted the best for you. But if you hadn't kept hassling me and forcing me to see what I was doing to myself and to you . . . I don't know. . . . It could have taken me forever."

"I've got more faith in you than that." *Do I?* she asked herself. There were so many times during the past eight months when she had felt like telling him to forget it, when she had wished they had never met, when she had wished she didn't have to deal with him at all. And she had doubted his faith in himself, too, wondering if he was as strong as she always imagined. But then, she had been weak in her own way, too.

"Perhaps being strong is being fragile, too," she said.

"What?"

"Oh, I don't know. I guess that doesn't make much sense, does it?"

"Sort of." He was quiet for a moment, absorbing her profile, the intensity of her nutmeg-brown eyes, wanting to kiss her. He took her chin in his hand and turned her face toward him, gently brushing her lips with his. "I love you, Kelly. Don't forget that," he whispered huskily.

The sensations that he thought he'd never have again blossomed in a long, searching kiss, and holding her, he vowed silently to never let her go again.

Scott's breath fluttered against her ear, and she felt at home in his arms.

"I love you, too," she said.

"If I'm never normal, will you still love me?"

Kelly giggled. "You never *were* normal."

They both laughed, at ease with each other. Scott held her tightly to him, so that she didn't see the tears dripping out of the corners of his eyes. *So, big, tough guy — even you have to cry once in a while.* The immensity of the moment was enough to crush a guy.

"Thanks for sticking by me," he breathed into Kelly's ear.

But she didn't need to be told . . . the loving fervor of his warm embrace told her everything she ever wanted to hear, and Scott said the rest. "The doctors say with hard work I'll walk normaly in another year or so. I'm going to be okay again. I know it."

Kelly pressed her face against his. "I know it, too. Anyway, we'll be together."

SUNFIRE ®

Read all about the fascinating young women who lived and loved during America's most turbulent times!

☐ MM32774-7	#1 AMANDA	Candice F. Ransom	$2.95
☐ MM33064-0	#2 SUSANNAH	Candice F. Ransom	$2.95
☐ MM33156-6	#4 DANIELLE	Vivian Schurfranz	$2.95
☐ MM33241-4	#5 JOANNA	Jane Claypool Miner	$2.95
☐ MM33242-2	#6 JESSICA	Mary Francis Shura	$2.95
☐ MM33239-3	#7 CAROLINE	Willo Davis Roberts	$2.95
☐ MM33433-6	#9 MARILEE	Mary Francis Shura	$2.95
☐ MM33381-X	#10 LAURA	Vivian Schurfranz	$2.95
☐ MM33410-7	#11 EMILY	Candice F. Ransom	$2.95
☐ MM33615-0	#13 VICTORIA	Willo Davis Roberts	$2.95
☐ MM33688-6	#14 CASSIE	Vivian Schurfranz	$2.95
☐ MM33686-X	#15 ROXANNE	Jane Claypool Miner	$2.95
☐ MM41468-2	#16 MEGAN	Vivian Schurfranz	$2.75
☐ MM41438-5	#17 SABRINA	Candice F. Ransom	$2.75
☐ MM42134-4	#18 VERONICA	Jane Claypool Miner	$2.75
☐ MM40049-5	#19 NICOLE	Candice F. Ransom	$2.25
☐ MM42021-6	#20 JULIE	Vivian Schurfranz	$2.50
☐ MM40394-X	#21 RACHEL	Vivian Schurfranz	$2.50
☐ MM43127-7	#22 COREY	Jane Claypool Miner	$2.75
☐ MM40717-1	#23 HEATHER	Vivian Schurfranz	$2.50
☐ MM43133-1	#24 GABRIELLE	Mary Francis Shura	$2.75
☐ MM41000-8	#25 MERRIE	Vivian Schurfranz	$2.75
☐ MM41012-1	#26 NORA	Jeffie Ross Gordon	$2.75
☐ MM41191-8	#27 MARGARET	Jane Claypool Miner	$2.75
☐ MM41207-8	#28 JOSIE	Vivian Schurfranz	$2.75
☐ MM41416-X	#29 DIANA	Mary Francis Shura	$2.75
☐ MM42043-7	#30 RENEE	Vivian Schurfranz	$2.75
☐ MM42015-1	#31 JENNIE	Jane Claypool Miner	$2.75

Available wherever you buy books, or use this order form.

Scholastic Inc., P.O. Box 7502, 2931 East McCarty Street, Jefferson City, MO 65102

Please send me the books I have checked above. I am enclosing $ _____
(please add $2.00 to cover shipping and handling). Send check or money-order—no cash or C.O.D.s please.

Name _____

Address _____

City _____ State/Zip _____

Please allow four to six weeks for delivery. Offer good in U.S.A. only. Sorry, mail orders are not available to residents of Canada. Prices subject to change.   SUN 890